Elle Woods

Beach Blonde

Elle Woods

Beach Blonde

Based on the character
created by Amanda Brown

Story by Natalie Standiford

HYPERION PAPERBACKS FOR CHILDREN
New York

First Edition

1 3 5 7 9 10 8 6 4 2

Printed in the United States of America
Library of Congress Cataloging-in-Publication Data on file

ISBN 0-7868-3844-2

Visit www.hyperionbooksforchildren.com

Elle Woods

Beach Blonde

Chapter 1

"WELCOME TO Seal Beach, my favorite place in the world," Hunter said. "You're going to love it."

He pulled his Mercedes convertible into a spot off the coast road. Elle Woods sat beside him in the front seat, her Chihuahua, Underdog, in her lap. Elle's best friend, Laurette Smythe, and Laurette's boyfriend, Darren Kidd, sat crammed in the tiny backseat.

Hunter Perry had been Elle's boyfriend for a month, ever since the Beverly Hills High School Senior Prom. Now school was over, Hunter had graduated, and summer was here. Elle, petite and blonde, looked proudly at her handsome new boyfriend, a black-haired, blue-eyed star athlete. She was crazy about him, and she could hardly believe he was hers.

"Elle," Laurette said. "You can't stare at Hunter all the time. Sometimes you need to take in the world around you. And this is one of those times."

Hunter grinned, took Elle by the chin, and turned her head toward the beach. She gasped.

"It's the most beautiful beach I've ever seen!" she cried. "And it's not even crowded."

Elle was a lifelong Los Angeles girl, a Californian through and through. She was used to swimming in her own backyard pool, but when she went to the beach, it was usually Santa Monica or Venice, where mobs of strollers and people gathered to show off their figures. There was food, there were Rollerbladers, there were freaks and tourists. It was like a circus.

But this was different. This was a surfer's paradise. The sun sat high in the sky over the sparkling water. Way out in the ocean, big, blue-green waves curled into tubes and dissolved into foam on the fine, beige sand. About a dozen surfers in bikinis and board shorts bobbed in the sea or lounged on the sand, waiting for the perfect wave. To the left of the surfers' beach, a few hundred yards in the distance, Elle saw a rocky cove. A shiny black rock with white spots seemed to flop into the water and disappear.

"Hey! Those rocks are moving!" Elle said.

"Those aren't rocks," Hunter said. "At least, not all of them are. They're seals. That's a rookery, or nesting ground, for the Pacific harbor seal. The babies were just born a month or two ago." He took a pair of binoculars from the glove compartment and handed them to Elle. She peered through them. She saw a white face with big, brown eyes and perky whiskers.

"They're adorable!" Elle held the binoculars for Underdog so he could see the seals. "Look, Underdog! Aren't they cute?" The Chihuahua didn't appear to be impressed, but then, it was hard to read his expression behind his dark glasses. He was looking very chic in his Hawaiian-print bandana and miniature Ray-Bans. "I want to go see them," Elle said, turning back to Hunter.

"Humans aren't allowed to go within a hundred feet of the seals," Laurette said. "By law. For the seals' protection."

"But you can always see them from here," Hunter said. "And sometimes from out on the water, when you're riding on top of an especially good curl."

"Let's go down and check out the scene," Darren

said. "I think my buddy Pablo is here.

The foursome hopped out of the car, careful not to hit their heads on Hunter's sky-blue surfboard, which had a red-and-yellow stripe down the middle and was strapped to the top of the car. Elle adjusted her new Gucci sunglasses and headed toward the beach in her gingham top and yellow shorts, Underdog riding along in her basket purse. Underneath her clothes she wore a new side-tied bikini she'd just bought at Calvin Klein. Laurette's vintage 1950s bathing suit had a flippy little skirt and could have doubled as a minidress, which was how she wore it, topped with a straw hat and heart-shaped sunglasses. Darren looked good next to her in his olive trunks and red T-shirt with the logo of one of his favorite local bands, Ribsy, printed on the front.

Hunter looked as though he belonged on the beach—which he did. He was the only real surfer of the four. He wore a T-shirt that said SUNRISE SURF SHACK and blue-flowered board shorts. Skillfully, he unstrapped his board and carried it toward the knot of surfers on the shore.

Darren had done some surfing but was more of a skater boy; and Laurette had tried surfing once or twice but didn't have much aptitude for it. Elle, on the other hand, had never surfed at all.

Her father, Dr. Wyatt Woods, a well-known Beverly Hills plastic surgeon, had tried to get her to surf when she was younger, but at the time she'd been too interested in designing dollhouses. Anyway, her mother, Eva, didn't think surf fashions were the way to go for her little princess. Not that Elle had looked much like a princess in those days; she cared more about making jewelry and other crafts than about what she wore. It was, as her mother liked to say, The Dark Ages: Elle's Mousy Brown Period.

But that was all over now. Elle was sixteen. She'd just finished her sophomore year of high school. To get Hunter to notice her, she had transformed the entire Beverly Hills High cheerleading squad, varsity basketball team, and marching band from dull to amazing. She'd tossed out her baggy clothes and started dressing beyond fashionably. She'd dolled up her beloved Underdog in cute little sweaters, gotten regular manicures, and, most important of all, gone blonde. Her grateful mother had called that happy new period The Enlightenment.

"Hunter!" the surfers cheered when they reached the shore. "Dude, get out there! Surf's up!"

"Hey, all!" Hunter squinted into the sun as the surfers gathered around. He took Elle's hand and introduced her, Laurette, and Darren to the surf crowd. "This is Aquinnah, Clive, Pablo, and Brett."

The surfers said friendly hellos, except for Clive, who said, "G'day," in a warm Australian accent.

Pablo clasped Darren's hand. "Hey, man, welcome to the brotherhood of surfers." Pablo played bass in Darren's band, Warp Factor 5, and was always trying to get him to give up skateboarding in favor of surfing.

"Watch it," Aquinnah said. "There are sisters here, too, you know."

Brett said, "Dude, you still a goofy foot?"

"You know it," Hunter said.

Elle checked Hunter's feet. They looked like their usual long, lean, beautiful selves to her.

"'Goofy foot' means right foot forward," Hunter explained, noticing Elle's questioning look. "I lead with my right foot when I surf."

"A lot of the greats do," Aquinnah said.

"Yeah, but a lot of them don't," Brett said. "You stick your aerial yet?"

"I've been working on it," Hunter said modestly.

"What are you talking about? I saw you stick one a few weeks ago," Clive said.

"I'll believe it when I see it," Brett said. "Come on, I'll race you to the break."

"In a minute," Hunter said. "I want to say hello to Sunrise."

He led Elle to a small shack decorated with plastic flowers and Christmas lights. A hand-painted sign read:

SUNRISE SURF SHACK
❀ **board gear**
❀ **snacks**
❀ **cold drinks**
❀ **good vibes**
❀ **healing hands**

"Elle, this is Sunrise," said Hunter. A stocky, well-muscled, and deeply tanned young woman grinned warmly at Elle. Her long, wavy brown hair was flecked with gold and topped with a wreath of wildflowers. She wore a batik sarong, and her fingers and toes were covered with rings.

"This is my girlfriend, Elle," Hunter said. Elle shivered with pleasure at hearing him call her his girlfriend. Their relationship was still so new that she got chills every time he said the word.

"Very cool to meet you," Sunrise said, "although

I think we may have actually met before."

"Really?" Elle said. She tried to remember where she might have met Sunrise before, but her mind drew a blank.

"In a past life," Sunrise said. "We were the sisters of a king in ancient Siam. You may not remember. Sometime I'll hypnotize you and see if it comes back."

"That would be great," Elle said. If she'd ever been a Siamese king's sister, she thought, she'd like to know about it.

A loud cry came from the water's edge, and Elle turned around just in time to see a girl in a plaid bikini tumble off her surfboard and get bonked in the head.

"I never say things like this," Sunrise said, "but this girl has driven me to say it: why doesn't she just give up?"

Hunter laughed but didn't say anything. The girl dragged her board out of the water, tripping over someone's misplaced beach sandal on the way. Elle recognized her immediately. It was her class-mate Chessie Morton.

Chessie dropped her board on the sand and came over to say hello.

"Hi, Chessie," Elle said. "What are you doing

here? I didn't know you surfed."

"Elle!" Chessie said. "It's Francesca, remember?"

Elle—and everyone else—had been calling her Chessie since second grade, but at the beginning of sophomore year she'd suddenly started insisting on her full name, Francesca. It didn't take. No one called Chessie "Francesca" except Chessie herself, when she remembered.

"I never thought I'd see *you* here," said Chessie. "It's kind of a secret, exclusive beach. Just for serious surfers. My brother Brett introduced me to it."

Elle looked toward the water, where a guy stood preening, showing off his biceps to a couple of girls. So that was Chessie's brother, Brett, she thought. The hypercompetitive one. It figured.

"I've never been here before," Elle explained. "Hunter brought me."

Chessie, a square-shouldered blonde, beamed up at Hunter. She'd always had a crush on him, and Elle knew it. But then, most girls at Beverly Hills had crushes on Hunter. Elle was used to it.

"Hi, Hunter," Chessie said. "I guess you brought Elle along to *watch* you surf? I can't really see her getting far in that bathing suit." She swept her eyes dismissively across Elle's bikini.

"Why?" Elle asked. "What's wrong with it?"

"Those ties will come undone in two seconds in that rough water," Chessie said. "Of course, maybe that's what you *want* to happen."

"No, of course not!" Elle said.

Chessie glanced over at Laurette, who had just joined the group. "At least there's no danger of *her* suit coming off," Chessie said, nodding at Laurette's vintage suit. "You'd need a crowbar to pry that thing off. I think I saw a picture of my great-great-great-grandmother swimming in a suit like that. In about 1904."

"Vintage suits are very chic now," Elle said. "They're making a big comeback."

"I guess you need to cover a lot of skin when you've got a figure like Laurette's," Chessie said.

What was that supposed to mean? Elle thought. Laurette wasn't skinny, but she had a great, curvy, voluptuous figure. Maybe Chessie meant she needed support for her curves.

Elle would have hated to think Chessie was insulting her friend.

"At least my suit doesn't hang halfway to my knees when it gets wet," Laurette shot back. Chessie self-consciously pulled her bikini bottoms up. They did sag a little in the back.

"Well, I'm going back out there," Chessie said.

"Come in with me and do some damage, Hunter?"

"Be out there soon," Hunter said.

"Did you bring a rubber duckie for Elle?" Chessie said.

"He didn't," Elle said. "But now that you mention it, it would be fun to have water wings."

"You won't need them," Hunter said. "I'm going to teach you to surf."

"And I'll help," Sunrise said. "I'm a wicked good teacher."

"I can't wait," Elle said. And she *was* very excited. But she was kind of scared, too. She watched Aquinnah and Clive climb up on their boards and zip across waves three times taller than they were. The waves crashed noisily on the shore, yet somehow Clive and Aquinnah avoided crashing with them. But how? That was the question. Elle couldn't imagine ever being able to do something like that. But that wouldn't stop her from trying.

Hunter took her hand. "Come on, Elle. Let's have our first lesson."

"You know, I could use a few lessons myself, Hunter," Chessie said.

"I bet you could," Laurette muttered, barely under her breath.

"You can watch me teach Elle, if you want,"

Hunter said. "But for now, I'm her private tutor."

Hmmm . . . private tutor. Elle liked the sound of that. Maybe surfing would be fun after all.

He dropped his board on the sand and showed Elle how to stand on it. Turned out she was a goofy foot . . . just like him.

Chapter 2

"DARLING, WHAT is that blotch on your nose?" Eva Woods asked.

Elle strolled past her mother in a bikini top and board shorts. She was barefoot, with her long blonde hair hastily knotted in a tangle on top of her head. She opened the refrigerator and reached for the orange juice. Kicking the fridge door shut, she touched the tip of her nose. A thick, greasy, white cream came off on her finger.

Eva approached her with a wet paper towel in one hand. "I think you forgot to wash off your cold cream this morning."

"It's not cold cream," Elle said. "It's zinc oxide. You know, like lifeguards wear. To protect my nose from the sun." Elle had seen Aquinnah wearing it that first day at Seal Beach. Elle was still pale, but she thought the zinc-tipped nose looked sporty.

"But, sweetheart, I bought you that lovely new sunblock," Eva said. "It was very expensive, and it must be good. It's French."

"That's not enough," Elle said. "I'm in and out of the water all day, and the sun's so strong at the beach. Do you want my nose to turn red and fall off?"

"Of course not, sweetie," Eva said. "I just want you to look nice. Not like a circus clown who missed a spot when taking off his makeup. You wouldn't go to the Galleria like that, would you?"

"Get hip, Eva," Wyatt Woods, Elle's father, said. "My pink pussycat has become a surf honey. The surf crowd is its own world, with its own style, even its own lingo." He rubbed the top of Elle's head, further tangling and mussing her hair.

"That's another thing," Eva said, staring at Elle's hair. "It's so salty and tangled! Just let me run a comb through it. Give me five minutes—"

Elle batted her mother away. "Mom, don't worry about it. Nobody at the beach cares how my hair looks. If it's not bleached out and messy, it means you haven't been surfing enough."

"I'll make a special conditioner for you," Zosia Wytzowski, the Woodses' maid, offered. She was famous for her homemade cosmetics and beauty treatments. She loved to tell Elle stories about her girlhood in Poland in the old days, when they couldn't get the cosmetics they wanted, so they learned to make their own. "Olive oil, egg yolk, avocado, and a few secret ingredients. It can detangle a hornet's nest and soften the most salt-encrusted locks."

Elle touched her hair. She was kind of proud of the way it had taken on the light, streaky surfer look so quickly.

"Maybe Bibi can do something with that streakiness," Eva said.

"Good idea," Elle said. "I'll call her today." Bibi was Elle's manicurist, hair colorist, and informal therapist and spiritual adviser. Elle was happy to have any excuse to visit Bibi.

"And it's nice to see you in a good Calvin bikini, but do you have to wear those baggy shorts around?" Eva said. "I wouldn't walk around Bel Air that way, dear. What will people say?"

"They'll probably just say Elle Woods is going surfing," Elle said.

"My daughter, a little grommet," Wyatt said, sucking on his pipe. "I flirted with the surf life, briefly, back in the sixties. It was a wild time—hot rods, longboards, the Beach Boys and 'Good Vibrations,' hanging ten . . ."

"Oh, Wyatt, you never did those things," Eva said.

"I did so," Wyatt insisted. "Didn't I, Bernard?"

"You certainly did, sir." Bernard was the family butler. He hadn't known the Woods family back in the sixties, but part of his job was to support Wyatt in any disagreement with his wife—at least Wyatt considered it part of his job. "Oh, yeah. You were gnarly, king of the dawn patrol."

"See?" Wyatt said.

"Oh, don't be ridiculous," Eva said.

"I believe you, Dad," Elle said. Deep down, she knew it was all a fantasy. It wasn't easy to picture the pipe-smoking Dr. Woods as a beach boy. But Elle figured even her parents had to have been teenagers once. It was hard to accept, but it could be true.

"Thank you, pussycat," Wyatt said. "We're made of the same stuff, you and I. The sun, the sea, the salt air . . . We live and breathe it."

"Oh, puh-leez," Eva said.

The doorbell rang, and Bernard went to answer

it. A minute later he reappeared and said to Elle, "Hunter's here. I told him you'd be ready in a minute."

"Thanks, Bernard." Elle started for her room to get her beach gear. She'd just bought an adorable new surfboard—pink with a yellow-and-white daisy on it—and she couldn't wait to put it to the test.

"Oooh! I'll go say hello," Eva said. "Take your time, Elle." She tripped out to the living room in her feathered, spike-heeled mules to see Hunter. Eva loved him and was thrilled to see Elle dating him. She often told Elle how proud she was that she'd snagged the cutest boy in Beverly Hills—and one of the richest, too.

"Nice young man," Wyatt said approvingly as he went to join Eva and Hunter. "I knew his father at Princeton."

Her parents were fawning over Hunter when Elle entered the living room.

"Let's roll, goofy foot," Hunter said. "I heard the waves are rockin' today."

"If the waves are rockin', don't come a-knockin'," Wyatt said.

Everyone stared at him.

"Dad, what does that even mean?" Elle finally asked.

Wyatt shrugged. "I guess my surf lingo's a little rusty."

"I'm ready to go," Elle said. She waved to her parents, jumped into Hunter's car, and they were off to the beach.

Chapter 3

ELLE SAW Darren's beat-up red Plymouth parked in the turnoff when she and Hunter pulled in at Seal Beach. "Oh, good," she said. "Darren and Laurette are here."

Darren sat alone on a rock, far from the surfers, playing guitar. Laurette sat on a beach blanket with a guitar of her own. Sunrise was teaching her how to play.

The waves were breaking far from the shore and were so beautiful Hunter couldn't resist going right in to catch a few. While he and his friends performed what looked to Elle like magic tricks on the water, she sat down with Laurette and Sunrise.

"Why is Darren sitting over there all by himself?"

Elle asked. "Is everything okay with him?"

"He's working on new songs for his band, and he doesn't want anyone to hear them until they're ready," Laurette said. "He's so into his band."

"I'm teaching Laurette some old Dick Dale surf tunes," Sunrise said. "She's picking it up fast. Soon she'll be good enough to play with Darren."

"If he'll let me," Laurette said. "I'm not sure he will. He treats his band like it's his private boys' club or something. Like he has to guard it from intruders who will ruin it."

"You'd never ruin it," Elle said. "And anyway, it's called Warp Factor Five, and there are only four of them. They need another member."

"That's what I think," Laurette said. "Maybe it's a boy thing. You know. The rawk." She pronounced "rock" in Darren's hipster drawl. Elle and Sunrise laughed.

Hunter came out of the water dripping and wedged his board in the sand. "Ready for another lesson, Elle?" he asked.

"Ready." Elle picked up her new board, and she and Hunter moved a few yards away.

"We'll practice your stance and the pop-up a few more times, and then we'll paddle out," Hunter said.

"Okay," Elle said. She was nervous about paddling out. She didn't feel ready. The waves looked awfully big. As she looked at them she saw Chessie, arms flailing, wipe out and get pounded by a major wave.

"Don't worry about her," Hunter said. "Just keep practicing your moves on the sand, and you'll be okay. You're doing well, I promise."

When the lesson was over, the hard-core surfers broke for lunch. They sat at the Surf Shack's lunch counter, and Sunrise served everyone sandwiches and veggie burgers. Laurette finished her sandwich and had a Fudgsicle.

"You're having a Fudgsicle?" Chessie asked her. She pronounced the word "Fudgicle," without the *s*, which Elle knew would bug Laurette, a stickler for linguistic correctness. "I wouldn't have thought that was on your diet."

"It's Fudg*sicle*," Laurette said. "And I'm not on a diet."

"You're not?" Chessie said. "Oh. Sorry. I just assumed you were."

"Wrong, as usual," Laurette said.

"You were hot out there, dude," Clive said, sitting down near Hunter and the others.

"Yeah, almost as good as me," Brett said. "I

hated to come in, but a man's got to eat."

"Did you see me?" Chessie said. "I rode toes on the nose."

Brett laughed. "Yeah, and then you pearl-dived face first into the foam."

Toes on the nose? Pearl-dived? Elle had no idea what they were talking about. But she decided not to ask too many questions. She felt out of place as it was with her lack of a tan and her inability to surf.

"It's okay, Chessie," Aquinnah said. "Everybody sucks in the beginning. I really bit it when I first started. Of course, I was only four, but—"

"She's right, Elle," Chessie said, brushing the comment off. "You should listen to her. It's okay to suck in the beginning. Don't worry if you're not as good as we are right away."

"Uh, yeah," Aquinnah said, confused.

Elle didn't say anything.

They wolfed down their food. Up by the road, a car pulled into the turnoff and stopped. Elle looked up. It was a chauffeur–driven black limousine with a shiny, expensive-looking surfboard strapped to a rack on the top.

"I don't think I've ever seen a surf rack on top of a limo before," Elle said.

"You haven't met Nica Saunders before," Aquinnah said. "Rich girl extraordinaire. Her daddy buys her all the latest gear."

"She's not bad, though," Pablo said.

"Anybody'd be good if they got private lessons from Kip Carter," Brett said.

"Who's Kip Carter?" Elle asked.

"He's a famous Hawaiian surf champ," Hunter said. "Nica's father actually sends her to Hawaii to train with him on school breaks."

"You'd think they'd want her to be home with them at least once in a while," Aquinnah said, "since most of the year she's at boarding school. And I don't mean *surf* boarding school." Elle was the only one who laughed at her pun.

"Maybe they don't like having her around," Brett suggested.

Chessie punched him in the arm. "Shut up! She's my friend."

"Oh, she is not," Brett said. "You wish."

"Why wouldn't they want her around?" Elle asked. "Is something wrong with her?"

"You'll see," Aquinnah said.

"She's not hard-core," Pablo said. "That's my only real problem with her. She's buying her way into the scene."

"Or her daddy is," Aquinnah said.

"What's wrong with that?" Chessie said. "She's got all the right gear, all the right moves, and she's super pretty . . . what else do you want?"

"A little heart," Aquinnah said. "A little soul."

"Surfing isn't just about gear," Pablo said. "It's a way of life."

A pretty girl, tall, slim, and tan, with wavy red hair, sauntered down the hill with her board tucked under one arm and a chic straw beach bag under the other. "Hey, there," she called to the gang at the Surf Shack. "How are they breaking today?"

Chessie jumped up. "Hi, Nica!" she cried too loudly. "Is that a new beach bag? I love it!"

"You missed a wicked morning," Clive said. "But the waves are still rolling in."

Nica took off her jeans and tank top. She was wearing an adorable red-and-white-checked bikini that fit her perfectly. Her board gleamed; it was gold and silver with black trim. She picked it up and ran gracefully into the water. Elle watched her paddle out, pop up, and sail over the first big wave that came along.

"Wow, she's good," Elle said. "She makes it look so easy."

"And she looks so good doing it," Clive said.

"Clive!" Aquinnah playfully slapped his arm.

"I'm just saying . . . " Clive said.

Hunter tossed his empty paper plate into the trash. "Who's up for another ride? Come on, Elle. Let's paddle out and see what you can do."

"Okay," Elle said. The veggie burger in her stomach seemed to be riding a wave of its own. "But remember, it's my first time in the water."

"Don't worry, love," Clive said. "We've all been there."

"You're going in the water in *that*?" Chessie asked, pointing at Elle's bathing suit.

Elle looked down at her second new bikini. This time she'd been careful not to wear one that tied; instead she had worn a bandeau top and cute bottoms decorated with little buttons on the front. "What's wrong with it?"

"Nothing," Chessie said. "It's cute. I mean, no serious surfer would ever wear it, but it's your choice. . . ."

Elle felt less confident than ever. "She's probably just trying to psych you out," Laurette whispered. "Though I can't say that for sure, since I know nothing about surfing."

Hunter took her hand. "You'll be fine. Let's go."

With Hunter holding her hand, Elle felt as if she

could have done anything. She nodded.

They grabbed their boards. He lashed hers to her right ankle and led her into the water. The waves weren't so high anymore. Elle and Hunter struggled past the shore break, and he showed her how to lie on her board and paddle out to the lineup, where the surfers waited to catch the next wave.

As soon as Elle lay her stomach on her board, she knew why her suit was all wrong. The buttons on the front pressed into her skin. They hurt, and they'd leave marks for sure, if not bruises. Oh, well, live and learn. She'd save this suit for poolside from now on. Of course, if she wiped out and killed herself on her first day of actual surfing, a few bruises wouldn't matter much.

When they got to the lineup, Elle and Hunter stopped and sat on their boards, waiting with the others for a good ride. A small wave was headed their way. "Okay, Elle," Hunter said. "This is a good one to start with. When I say go, start paddling and pop up. Ready . . . go!"

Hunter gave her a push. Elle furiously paddled through the water on her board. The wave caught up with her, and she tried to stand up on her board. But the rush of water dragged on her strapless top and nearly pulled it off. She reached up to keep it from falling to her hips, thus letting go of the board. It flew along with the wave, the leash tugging at her ankle, as Elle was pulled under and finally dragged to shore. Luckily, she wasn't hurt.

"Good try, Elle!" Hunter called. "Good first try!"

Elle paddled back out to the lineup. "Your top almost turned into a belt," Chessie said. "I had no idea you were such an exhibitionist."

"Next time, let your top go," Clive said. "And we'll all be better off."

"Clive, you're such a dog," Aquinnah said. "But he's right, Elle—better to let your bathing suit fall off than to fall off your board."

"I'll wear a better suit tomorrow," Elle said. If she had to worry about being naked in front of everybody, she'd never learn to surf. It was just too distracting. She vowed to stop off at a surf shop on her way home for a new bikini—a *surfing* bikini.

Chapter 4

"OKAY, YOU'VE almost got it," Hunter said. "One more try and I bet you'll be able to stand up."

Elle was back at the beach two days later in a new bathing suit, determined to master surfing if it killed her. She'd bought a one-piece sport suit that the guy at the surf shop had said was the best suit available. But what did a guy know—even a surf guy—about straps falling down and bottoms riding up? Nothing, as Elle was learning that day.

Elle paddled back to the lineup after yet another fall and waited for the next wave. "Don't worry," Hunter said. "Surfing is tricky. It takes time. You just started."

"I know," Elle said, adjusting her suit strap. "But I

feel like I'm not getting anywhere."

"You will," Hunter said. "I have faith in you—more than anyone else I know. If it can be done, you can do it. You can do anything."

Elle flushed with pleasure at the compliment. But there was no time for lovey-dovey stuff. A big wave roared toward them. Elle clutched her board nervously. "Let this one pass," Hunter said, to her relief. Elle let the wave swell underneath her. A few yards away she heard a whoop and saw Nica pop up on to her board and fly over the water, red hair trailing behind her like a flag.

"Hang ten!" Chessie shouted. She was in her usual spot, right behind Nica, and struggling to stand on her board. She managed it for a second, but was too far back, and the board popped out from under her. She fell with a smack into the churning water, then came up sputtering, shouting, "That was a great ride!"

Brett shook his head. "I can't believe that's my sister."

"Okay, Elle, here comes one," Hunter said. Elle watched the modest wave skip toward her. She gripped her board. "Start paddling!" Hunter shouted.

Elle paddled. She could feel the wave coming up behind her. For the first time, she had a sense of it. She was in perfect position, just ahead of the curl. As she popped up on to her board, she checked her stance: good. The wave pushed her along, but the bottom of her suit had ridden up uncomfortably when she jumped out of the water.

Don't think about it, she told herself. Just don't think about it.

But how could she not think about it when half of her butt was hanging out?

The next thing she knew, she wiped out.

"That was better!" Hunter shouted. "Almost!"

Almost, almost, Elle thought as she paddled back. He must be getting so tired of saying that. When will I ever get the hang of this?

"You actually got your feet on the board!" Chessie shouted. "That's the best you've ever done! Come on, Hunter, let's take the next one together."

Hunter checked with Elle. "Do you mind?"

She wanted him to have a good time and didn't want to hold him back. "It's okay," Elle said. "I'll take the next wave and catch up with you"— though she knew that was unlikely.

"She doesn't mind," Chessie said. "Elle knows better than to try to keep up with us hard–core wave riders."

Elle squinted across the water at Chessie. She

knew Chessie meant well. But sometimes Elle wished she'd just shut up. Luckily, the next wave took care of that, dumping Chessie face first into the water.

"Come on, Underdog, let's go for a walk." Elle threw a sarong over her bathing suit and a straw hat on her head. It had been a long, hard afternoon of surfing—or lack thereof.

"I'll come with you," Laurette said, putting her guitar away. "I'm so sick of playing scales. Feels like I'll never learn how to play."

"I hear you," Elle said. "My whole body is covered with bruises. My surfboard keeps finding new spots to hit me."

Elle and Laurette followed Underdog as he trotted along the beach in his tiny plaid swim trunks and wraparound sunglasses. They walked south, toward the seal rookery. Underdog skittered ahead and out of view. A few minutes later, Elle heard him barking.

"Something must be wrong," she said, hurrying toward the barking.

Underdog stood on one of the rocks that protected the seal cove, staring at something on the edge of the water. It was a small black seal with a few scattered white spots on its belly.

"Oh!" Elle cried. "It's adorable!"

"Totally," Laurette said. "But don't get too close. Remember the hundred-yard rule."

The seal flopped around in the surf, making a heartbreaking *maa maa* sound. Its puppylike face reminded Elle of Underdog's. She picked up her dog to keep him from getting too close to the seal and scaring it. "What do you think, Underdog?" she asked him. Underdog let out a single bark. Elle had a feeling he liked the seal.

"That's funny," Laurette said, looking around. "Wasn't there a whole seal colony here the other day?"

"That's right, there was," Elle said. "There were at least a dozen seals. Where'd they all go?"

"Maybe the mothers went out looking for food," Laurette said. "They'll probably come back soon."

"But what about all the other baby seals?" Elle said. "Where have they gone? They're called pups, right? Well, what if this pup has been abandoned?"

"I don't think a pup that young could take care of itself," Laurette said. "Maybe we'd better wait and make sure its mother comes back." Elle and Laurette sat down on the rock. They watched the seal play in the water.

"Do you think it's a boy or a girl?" Elle asked.

"I can't tell from here," Laurette said.

"I think it's a girl," Elle said. "I think Underdog has a little crush on her."

"I don't blame him," Laurette said. "I'm falling in love with her, too. Look at that little face."

The seal rolled in the surf, clapped her little fins together, and bobbed her head. It was almost as if she were dancing for them. Her dark eyes sparkled mischievously, and she had one round white spot over her left eye, like a polka dot.

"I love the way that white dot is set just off center," Elle said, "like when you wear your newsboy cap pulled over one eye."

"It's sassy," Laurette said.

"Yes, it's very sassy," Elle said. "Let's call her Sassy."

"All right," Laurette said, "but we probably shouldn't get too attached to her. Her mother might come back any minute."

Elle glanced at the sun, moving inevitably closer to the horizon to meet the ocean. "Do you think she'll come back before dark?"

"She has to," Laurette said. She leaned back against the rock and scratched Underdog's head. Underdog couldn't take his eyes off Sassy.

"Where's Darren today?" Elle asked. "Why didn't he come to the beach?"

"He had a band rehearsal," Laurette said. "Actually, we had a little fight."

"Oh, no. About what?"

"The band," Laurette said. Warp Factor 5 had recently played their first gig, thanks to Elle: the Beverly Hills High Senior Prom.

"They're so ambitious," Laurette said. "They really want to make it big. Playing the Prom was huge, but now they want to score a real gig. They want to play in front of people they didn't go to school with."

"I can understand that," Elle said.

"But Darren's obsessed with it," Laurette said. "It takes all his time. All he wants to do is rehearse. And he doesn't want anyone else around at re-hearsals. Not even me."

"In a way that makes a little sense," Elle said. "They have to focus. And he's so crazy about you you'd probably distract him."

"But they practice all the time," Laurette said. "I hardly ever get to see him. That doesn't seem like someone who's crazy about me. It's the most important thing in his life, and I feel left out of it."

"You're learning to play guitar," Elle said. "That's

one good way to spend more time with him."

"Well, I've always wanted to play guitar," Laurette said. "But now I'm extra motivated. I thought if I learned to play well enough, Darren might let me join the band. Or at least jam with them."

"Maybe he will," Elle said.

Laurette shook her head. "He won't even give me a chance. He already told me he doesn't want to have his girlfriend in the band with him. He says love and the rawk shouldn't mix. Can you believe that? It's so frustrating!"

"That *is* terrible," Elle said. "What goes better together than love and music? And I can think of lots of examples of couples who've played together."

"I've thrown them all at him. Sonny and Cher. He says they ended up divorced. Tina and Chris of Talking Heads. He says their love drove David Byrne away and ruined the band. Georgia and Ira of Yo La Tengo. He says nerd rock doesn't count. The Captain and Tennille. He says they suck."

"He's just wrong," Elle said.

"The thing is, when he's not obsessing about music, he's really sweet," Laurette said. "He could be a good boyfriend if he let his tender side come out more."

"He just needs to be softened up a little," Elle said. "I have an idea. Let's have a beach bonfire tonight! A romantic bonfire, right here on Seal Beach. Just the four of us: you and Darren and me and Hunter. We'll roast vegetarian hot dogs and marshmallows and look for shooting stars. . . ."

"Maybe we can even sing songs together," Laurette said. "I'll bring my guitar, and Darren and I can play, and we'll all sing along . . . and maybe he'll see what a good thing it can be."

"Perfect! I'll go home and pack a picnic dinner, and we'll all meet back here at nine tonight," Elle said. She looked at the sun, turning orange on the horizon. "It's going to be dark soon. Where is Sassy's mother?"

"I have a feeling she might not be coming back," Laurette said.

"But why not?" Elle cried. "How could she leave such an adorable pup all alone? What if some animal comes along and tries to eat her?"

"Maybe we'd better call the wildlife refuge." Laurette pulled her cell phone out of her beach bag. "They'll know what to do."

Laurette called the wildlife refuge, and a few minutes later a dark green pickup truck with the wildlife refuge logo on the door appeared.

"Are you the girls who called about the seal pup?" A short woman in a dark khaki uniform and baseball cap emerged from the truck and walked up to them. "I'm park ranger Paula Kramer, Malibu Wildlife Refuge."

Elle stood up to shake her hand. "I'm Elle Woods, seal rescuer. This is Laurette Smythe, also a seal rescuer, and Underdog, a seal lover."

Paula surveyed the scene. Sassy now sat forlornly on a rock, staring out to sea as if hoping for a glimpse of her missing mother. "You girls did the right thing in calling us. This is a real problem."

She walked the perimeter of the rookery, looking carefully at the sand and the water. "This is very strange. This was a thriving nesting area only a few days ago. Something must have driven all the seals away."

"What could have done it?" Elle asked.

"I don't know," Paula said. "The sand and the water look fine, as far as I can tell. I don't see anything that might disturb them. But something has, that's for sure. And I'm afraid the seals won't come back here as long as their nesting area is disturbed."

"Not even Sassy's mother?" Elle said.

"I take it you're referring to the seal pup?" Paula asked.

"We named her Sassy," Laurette said.

"I don't think Sassy's mother is coming back," Paula said. "Unless we find out what drove her away in the first place, and fix the problem."

"But what will happen to Sassy?" Elle asked.

"I'll have to take her to the wildlife refuge for now," Paula said. "She's too young to live on her own. We'll take good care of her."

"If the mother comes back, can Sassy go with her?" Laurette asked.

"Sure," Paula said, "if she comes back. I don't think that's too likely."

"Can we visit Sassy at the wildlife refuge?" Elle asked. "I think Underdog is in love with her."

"Sure, any time," Paula said. She went to her truck to get a special carrier for Sassy. It wasn't hard to catch the seal; she was too little to get very far on her own. Elle, Laurette, and Underdog watched sadly as Paula drove her away. Elle waved Underdog's paw for him.

"Poor Sassy," Elle said. She looked at the nesting area, empty except for the water, sand, and rocks. There were no more seals in the seal cove. It wasn't right. "I don't understand it. What could have disturbed the seal colony so much that they all left for good? Everything looks fine."

"It could be anything," Laurette said. "Bacteria in the water, a lack of food to eat, some kind of predator . . . Who knows?"

"It's getting dark," Elle said. "We'd better get back. We have to get ready for our bonfire tonight. Make sure Darren comes."

"He'll be there," Laurette said, "if I have to drag him out of his garage myself."

Chapter 5

"*BEACH BABY, beach baby, here on the sand . . .*"
Darren strummed his guitar as he, Elle, Hunter, and
Laurette sang summer songs all night long. The
bonfire cast a rosy glow on their faces. It was a
clear, still night. The moon gleamed on the water.
Their bellies were full of s'mores. Elle leaned
against Hunter, and he took her in his arms and
kissed her. They had music and each other. What
more could they want?

Darren put his guitar aside and gave Laurette a
squeeze.

Elle approved. "Isn't it fun to play music with
your friends, Darren?" she said. "With people you
care about?"

"Sure," Darren said.

"Just think how much fun it would be if Laurette played in Warp Factor Five with you."

"It would be lots of fun," Darren said.

Laurette brightened. The plan was working!

"But fun is fun, and business is business," Darren said. Laurette deflated. "They don't go together."

"Business?" Laurette said. "I thought it was the rawk."

"I have to take it seriously if I'm going to get anywhere," Darren said. "That means no fooling around. No girls."

"Isn't the whole point of being in a band to *get* girls?" Hunter said.

"Hey!" Elle bonked his chest with the back of her head to show him her disapproval. "You're not helping."

"Helping what?" Hunter asked.

Elle hadn't let him in on the plan. She was afraid he might not sympathize with Laurette's plight. Boys tended to stick together.

"The last thing the Factor needs is a Yoko," Darren said.

"A Yoko?" Laurette said. "You think Yoko Ono broke up the Beatles?"

"It's a theory," Darren said.

"Laurette would never be a Yoko," Elle said.

"I'm sure that's what Yoko said, too," Darren responded.

"Whatever," Laurette said.

"Let's go for a walk," Elle said to Hunter. She got to her feet and took Hunter's hand. "We won't be back for at least twenty minutes, so you have plenty of snuggle time," she told Darren and Laurette. "Or fight time, whichever you need more."

"Wait!" Darren cried. "Don't leave me alone with her! No-o-o-o!"

"Stop kidding around," Laurette said.

"You'll survive," Hunter said.

"You'd better hope so," Darren said. "You'll be sorry if you come back and find my lifeless body on the cold sand, and Laurette dancing around chanting some kind of evil voodoo rant."

"What are you talking about?" Elle said.

"He's just babbling," Laurette said. "You two take your walk."

Elle walked hand in hand with Hunter along the moonlit beach, the waves lapping gently at their feet. "You know something, Elle?" Hunter said softly. "So far this is the best summer I've ever had. And it's mostly because of you."

"Really?" Elle's heart swelled. Sometimes she still couldn't believe a handsome, popular, perfect guy like Hunter actually liked *her*. But it was true. There he stood beside her, holding her hand, telling her how she was making his summer good. It was better than a dream.

"Really," Hunter said. He stopped and leaned down to kiss her. He was quite a bit taller than she was, so kissing was sometimes a challenge. But it was a fun challenge.

They broke away from each other and started walking again. "Well, you and the wicked surf we've had this year," Hunter said. "Just kidding. It really is mostly you."

"I love surfing," Elle said. "I wish I could be as good at it as you are. You spend so much time trying to teach me, and I'm so hopeless. I don't want to hold you back. You should be free to shred the combers."

"'Combers'? That must be one of your dad's old terms," Hunter said. "You mean, 'swells'? Or maybe 'bombs'?"

"Sure . . . if you say so," Elle said. "I'm still working on my lingo. Sunrise is tutoring me in conversational surf talk."

"You could use a few more lessons," Hunter

said, laughing. "But you're not holding me back, Elle. I love teaching you to surf. You have to be patient—it takes time. I know you'll get it soon. In the meantime, you look so cute on your board, I don't mind waiting for you to catch on."

Elle giggled. He was so sweet.

"And at least you are not the official Seal Beach kook. That would be Chessie," Hunter said.

"Kook?" Elle said. "I haven't learned that one yet."

"You know, she can be annoying. And klutzy. Sometimes I wish she'd get out of my face. You know what I mean?"

"I do," Elle said, "but she means well. She can't help it that she's such a klutz. I mean, 'kook.'"

"She's been surfing for five years," Hunter said. "I'm afraid she's one person who's never going to get it."

They were walking south, toward the seal rookery—or what had once been the rookery. Elle spotted something glowing up ahead. A bright light. Where could it have been coming from? There were no buildings in that direction. There was nothing but beach.

"What's that?" she asked Hunter.

"I don't know," he said. "I've never seen a light like that here before."

They moved closer to investigate. There were several bright lights set up on the beach. It was almost as if someone were shooting a movie there. But a loud, grinding noise, and the presence of several large machines, made Elle realize it wasn't a movie. Unless it was a movie about trucks and digging—which she didn't imagine would do very well at the box office.

"It's just beyond the seal cove," Elle said. "It looks like they're digging, or building something."

Elle and Hunter ducked behind some rocks so they wouldn't be seen. Something told Elle that whoever was there and whatever they were doing, they wouldn't appreciate witnesses. The fact that they were working secretly at night kind of gave that away.

"It's some kind of construction site," Hunter said. "But there's no construction allowed here. This is all zoned for parkland. It's a wildlife preserve."

They moved closer, taking cover behind the rocks. The tide was out. Men in hard hats were installing pilings on the beach, in the shallows. When the tide rose, the pilings would be hidden. There would be no sign of the work.

"Look." Elle pointed at a pickup truck parked on the beach. "There's a name on the truck. I'm going to sneak up and see if I can read it."

Hunter held her by the arm. "Elle, don't. What if they see you? You could get into trouble."

"How? I'm not doing anything wrong," Elle said.

"No, but maybe *they* are," Hunter said. "And people don't like it when you catch them doing something wrong."

"Too bad for them." Elle wrested her arm from his grip. "You stay here. They're less likely to see me alone than the two of us. And I'm smaller, so I can hide more easily."

"Be careful!" Hunter whispered.

She crawled down the beach, ducking from rock to rock.

Elle crept up on the construction workers. There were only four or five of them, along with one dump truck and one pickup truck. Careful to stay out of the beam of the headlights, she huddled behind the nearby rocks. She could just make out the white printing on the side of the pickup truck's door: SAUNDERS DEVELOPMENT COMPANY.

Like a soldier dodging bullets, Elle made her way back to Hunter and safety.

"Did you see it?" he asked.

"It says *Saunders*," Elle said. "Isn't that Nica's last name?"

Hunter nodded.

"That's a funny coincidence," Elle said.

"If it *is* a coincidence," Hunter said.

They walked back to the bonfire, where they found Laurette and Darren happily singing "Summer Nights" from *Grease*. "You sound good together," Elle said. "Did you decide to let Laurette play with your band, after all, Darren?"

Laurette looked at Darren to see what his answer would be.

"No," Darren said. "I still say girls and rock don't mix."

"What about the Donnas?" Laurette said. "Or the Go-Go's?"

"You can bring up all the examples you want," Darren said. "I really like you, I think you're cute, and I want you around. Just not when I'm rehearsing with my band. The end."

Disappointment flickered across Laurette's face.

Elle felt sorry for her. Their plan hadn't worked. But they wouldn't give up. There must be some way to show Darren how wrong he was. Women and rock didn't mix? What century was he living in?

In the meantime, something more important had come up. "I think I know why the seals disappeared," Elle said. "There's some kind of construction going on near the nesting area."

Laurette stood up and stared down the beach. "I do see something down there, now that you mention it."

"Why are they working at night?" Darren asked. "Isn't that supposed to be a wildlife refuge?"

"I think so," Laurette said. "No one is supposed to build around there."

"That's what we've got to find out," Elle said. "And guess what? The company is called Saunders Development."

"Hmmm . . . Saunders . . . as in, Nica?" Laurette said. "Maybe she'll be able to explain what this is all about."

"We'll ask her tomorrow," Elle said. "Very nicely."

"And carefully," Laurette added.

Chapter 6

ELLE PULLED herself out of the foamy water, pushed her tangled, wet hair out of her face, and tried to shake the sand out of her suit after yet another wipeout.

"This is impossible," she muttered to herself. No matter what suit she wore, she always ended up with a seat full of sand, and nothing could get it all out.

"Elle, are you okay?" Chessie hurried up to her, her face full of feigned concern. "That looked like it really hurt!"

"Thanks for asking," Elle said. "Actually, I'm—"

Chessie turned away. "Look—Nica's here. Nica! Hi, Nica!" She hurried off to greet the lanky redhead, who had just been dropped off by her chauffeur.

"—okay," Elle finished.

Nica dropped her towel in the sand and hurried toward Elle with Chessie on her heels. "I saw that wipeout from the car," Nica said. "Are you all right?"

"I already asked her that," Chessie said. "She's fine. Wax up and come out to the lineup, Nica. The waves are rolling great today."

"In a minute," Nica said. "Elle, let me give you a little lesson. I think I can help you."

"Really? Thanks, Nica," Elle said.

"Just watching you has made me a better surfer, Nica," Chessie said. "But I'd love it if you'd give *me* a personal lesson, too."

"Maybe another day, Chessie," Nica said. "I'm not sure I can help you, though."

"Because I'm so good, right?" Chessie said. She wisely didn't wait around for an answer, but picked up her board and trotted back into the surf.

Elle was surprised. Until then, Nica hadn't really shown any interest in her. I guess people can change their minds, Elle thought.

Nica waxed her gleaming board, and Elle followed her out to the lineup. Elle was anxious to ask her what she knew about Saunders

Development Company, but this didn't seem to be the time. She saw Laurette sitting on her blanket with a book, watching them from under her big straw hat. Elle knew Laurette was waiting to hear what Nica would say; she gave her a little wave as if to say, *I know, I'm on it.*

When they reached the lineup, Nica said, "Let me see your pop-up."

Elle started out with her belly on the board. She popped up to a squat and then, wobbly, tried to stand. Her board sank beneath her, and she hopped off.

"Not bad," Nica said. "But I think you need practice balancing. Do you work the Indo board at home?"

"The what?" Elle asked.

"The Indo board. It's a little surfboard on a roller for practicing indoors—like a skateboard, with two wheels instead of four. If you practice standing on it and cross-stepping, I bet you'll improve faster."

"Thanks, Nica," Elle said. "I'll get one today."

"No problem," Nica said. "I definitely believe it's worth spending a lot of money on equipment. I buy everything I can get my hands on. Some of it's useful, some isn't. . . . But how will I know until I try it, right?"

"I guess," Elle said. Nica was being really nice to

her now. It was hard to ask a challenging question like, *Is someone in your family up to no good?*

"Here comes a good small wave," Nica said. "Take it, Elle!"

Elle paddled forward to catch the wave. As she popped up, the sand in her bikini bottoms scratched her hip. She reached down to wipe it away . . . and *splat!*

She came up for air to see Nica gliding past like a goddess on a seashell.

When they broke for lunch a while later, Elle saw her opportunity to confront Nica and took it. She sat down next to her at Sunrise's lunch counter.

Laurette sat next to Elle. She would have sat on Nica's other side, to up the intimidation factor, but Chessie had already snagged that spot.

"So, Nica," Elle began, "what does your father do for a living?"

"He's a developer," Nica said. "Why?"

It was hard to think of a delicate way to pry into Nica's personal family affairs, so Elle opted for the blunt approach. "Does he own Saunders Development Company?" she asked.

"Duh, that's our name. Of course. Why?"

"We had a bonfire here on the beach last night," Laurette said. "Elle and Hunter saw a truck from your father's company digging in the surf near the seal cove."

"We found the sweetest little baby seal near there yesterday," Elle said. "She'd been abandoned by her mother! All the other seals were gone. We had to call a park ranger to take her away."

"So?" Nica said.

"So—what is your father's company doing?" Laurette said. "The construction is driving the seals away. Seal rookeries are protected wildlife areas."

"Are you suggesting that my father's company is doing something illegal?" Nica asked.

"No, not exactly," Elle said. "We were just wondering what he *is* doing."

"I heard him mention this project," Nica said. "It's no big deal. He's just building a tiny dock and visitors' center near the rookery so scientists can study the seals. And people can come look at them without disturbing them—as you've obviously been."

"We never disturbed them!" Elle said.

"The state probably asked him to do it," Nica said. "When the center is built, people will appreciate the seals more, and the state can raise money to help save their habitat."

"That sounds very nice, but why does he have

to build this lovely little project at night?" Laurette asked.

Nica shrugged. "How should I know? Maybe he's so busy with bigger projects during the day that night is the only time he can work. Maybe he's taken this project on as a kind of charity work, and he can't afford to spend valuable daylight hours on it because he has other projects that bring in more money. Maybe he doesn't want to disturb the surfers here in the day. Whatever it is, it's not illegal. That's his motto."

Laurette raised an eyebrow. "That's his *motto*? 'Whatever it is, it's not illegal'? That's some motto. Truly inspirational."

"It's something like that," Nica said irritably. "What business is this of yours, anyway?"

"It's just that what you're saying doesn't make sense," Laurette said. Elle knew Nica was in for it. Laurette would grab the topic by the teeth and hang on like a bulldog. She hated it when things didn't make sense. "You say he's building something to help the seals, but just by building it he's already driven them away. How can he help them if they've fled in terror?"

"Look—my father would never do anything to hurt the environment," Nica said. "Maybe the seals have gone away, but that's just temporary. After the visitors' center is built, they'll come flooding back. They'll love it! Their nesting area will be better than before!"

"I don't see how," Laurette said. "How can you improve on nature?"

"Maybe Nica's father will decorate it nicely for them," Chessie said. "Or make some kind of safe, comfy tanks for them or something. How do you know what seals like? Who made you the expert?"

"I'm just being logical," Laurette said.

"You're accusing my father of hurting seals!" Nica stood up indignantly and tossed her half-eaten sandwich into the trash. "How dare you? I told you, whatever he's doing is legal and good, so just stop asking questions!"

Nica marched away.

"I can't believe you hurt Nica's feelings, all over a silly seal," Chessie said and trotted after her.

"Maybe Nica is right," Elle said. "Maybe the seals will come back after the construction is finished. I just hope it won't be too late for Sassy to get back with her mother by then."

"I don't think she's right," Laurette said. "There's something weird going on here. There's more to the story than Nica's letting on."

"She probably told us all she knows," Elle said, always eager to believe the best in people, especially when it came to someone who had just given her a good surfing tip.

"Maybe so," Laurette said. "I bet her father doesn't tell her everything."

"I'm going to find out," Elle said. "I've got to know the truth. I won't rest until Sassy is reunited with her mother."

"It's not going to be easy," Laurette said.

"That won't stop me," Elle said.

"It never does," Laurette said.

Chapter 7

ELLE TOOK the next day, Saturday, off from surfing to do a little research. The sky was somewhat overcast, anyway. As soon as she woke up she went straight to her computer and logged on. Underdog jumped up onto her lap.

She started at the beginning, typing *Seal Beach* in to a search engine. Once she got started she couldn't stop. One Web site led to another and another, but the more answers she found, the more questions she had.

First she looked up the state of California and confirmed that Seal Beach was zoned as parkland reserved for protected wildlife. No development was allowed there—none at all. So how had Nica's father gotten permission to build a visitors' center?

Then she found some articles in Malibu's community newspaper revealing that the state had been selling off small parcels of parkland to raise funds. The story was still under investigation, but the reporter wrote that the government was quietly changing the zoning laws to allow some development of protected areas. Government officials knew people would protest if they found out, so they tried to keep it quiet.

Elle double-checked Seal Beach's status: still protected. But what if the state *un*protected it? What would happen to the beautiful, quiet beach and the seal rookery?

She was still in her flannel puppy-print pajamas, glued to her laptop, when her father knocked on her bedroom door.

"Elle? Pussycat? Are you feeling all right?"

"Come in," Elle called distractedly.

Her father walked in, dressed in his usual Saturday outfit, tennis whites. "Don't you want some breakfast?" he asked. "Bernard made waffles."

Elle hardly heard him. She was busy reading about a woodland area in the northern part of the state. It had once been a protected habitat for owls, but the state had sold the land to a developer who built houses there. Now the owls were dying off, because they'd lost the trees they'd lived in and had nowhere else to go.

She glanced at the bed of pink velvet cushions Underdog loved so much. What if someone were to take it away from him? He'd be heartbroken. But she could always get him another one. For those owls it was worse. They had no new home to go to. There were very few places left where they could live. That was what was happening to Sassy and her mother and the other seals. If the seals lost Seal Beach, they might have to swim far away to find another decent place to live. One day there might be no seals left in all of southern California. Elle couldn't let that happen.

"Elle? What are you doing?" her father asked.

"Dad, let me ask you something—do you know anything about land developing?"

"You mean, buying, selling, building? Real estate?" Wyatt said.

Elle nodded.

"Are you kidding?" Wyatt said. "This is California. When you turn eighteen they give you a real-estate license along with your voting card."

"I guess I have a lot to learn before I turn eighteen, then," Elle said. "I'm trying to find out about our surfing spot, Seal Beach."

"Ah, yes. It's one of the last bits of undeveloped coastline in the area," Wyatt said. "Developers have been trying to get their hands on it for years. It's worth hundreds of millions of dollars. You just can't find pristine land like that around here anymore."

"But if it's protected, no one can touch it—right?" Elle said.

"Right," Wyatt said.

"Not even to build a visitors' center?"

"Well, maybe, if the state gives permission for that," Wyatt said.

"Thanks, Dad." She turned back to her computer.

"I see you're in one of your obsessive moods," Wyatt said. "I'll have Bernard bring you some waffles."

"Thanks, Dad." When Elle got caught up in a project, she had trouble letting go. She worked on it and worked on it until she was finished—or until her eyes felt as if they were going to dry up in her head.

Only a few months earlier, Elle had given herself a crash course in basketball and cheerleading until she knew so much she was practically able to coach both teams. And once, when she was much younger, she had spent an entire week sewing gold sequins on fabric to build a glittery nightclub for her Malibu Barbie, who, Elle had decided, was desperate to become the next big singing star.

But this was different. This was more important than the ambitions of Barbie or even the fate of sports in Beverly Hills. A life was at stake—Sassy's life.

Elle finally found the Saunders Development Company Web site. She wanted to see what their other wildlife visitors' centers looked like. Up popped a big photo of a grinning, ruddy man with graying red hair and a double chin. A banner read: OUR FOUNDER, FRED SAUNDERS. The site showcased all of the firm's latest projects: a mall in Orange County; a huge tract of mansions in the Valley; an apartment building in downtown L.A.; condos near San Diego with a marina attached; and more shopping centers and houses. But not one wildlife center. Nothing even similar to a wildlife center. As far as Elle could tell, Fred Saunders had no interest in wildlife whatsoever.

Elle's mother barged in. "Darling, don't you have an appointment with Bibi today?" She scanned her disheveled daughter's sun-bleached, uncombed hair, chipped fingernails, and unwashed face.

Elle got up and glanced in the mirror. "I do. Which is good—I look like a wild animal in puppy pajamas," she said. "I'll be ready in five."

Not only did Elle need some serious grooming, she needed help and advice—or at least comfort. And Bibi never let her down.

"Come on, Underdog," Elle said. "We're going to see Mommy." Bibi's Chihuahua, Kitty, was Underdog's mother. Underdog jumped into Elle's bag, ready to go. He cherished the visits to the Pamperella Salon as much as Elle did.

Chapter 8

KITTY NUZZLED Underdog as Elle sat at Bibi Barbosa's manicure table. Bibi, a pretty young Texan with long brown hair, filed Elle's nails. She was wearing a fire-engine red dress that wrapped around her body as if it were made of bandages. "That poor little seal," she said. "All alone in the world without her mother! It's just heartbreaking."

"I wish I knew where the other seals went," Elle said. "Maybe we could take Sassy to her mother, wherever she is. Though I'd rather have them all close by at Seal Beach. That's their real home."

"They could be anywhere," Bibi said. "I agree with you, Elle—something funny is going on. Construction that happens only at night? That's too weird to be completely legal."

"But it isn't illegal, is it?" Elle said.

"I guess not," Bibi said. "They do roadwork on the freeway at night."

"I need to find proof that Mr. Saunders is up to no good," Elle said.

"Did you say, 'Saunders'?" Bibi said. "Fred Saunders?"

"Yes," Elle said. "He's the developer. His daughter, Nica, surfs with us. Do you know him?"

"No, but I know more than I'd like to *about* him," Bibi said. "His wife, Marla, is one of my steady clients. She's a very nice woman, but all she does is complain about her husband."

"What does she say?" Elle asked.

"She says he works until all hours of the night," Bibi told her quietly. "Sometimes he doesn't get home until dawn. He tells her he is working."

"Hmmm . . ." Elle said.

"What could he be doing at work in the middle of the night?" Bibi said.

"Building illegally on protected state parkland, that's what," Elle said. "Maybe Mrs. Saunders and I can help each other out."

"Actually . . ." Bibi glanced around the salon. "Saturday is her facial day. She might be here right now." She stared at a woman lying back in a chair in a glass room, her face covered with a green cream. "I think that's her, over there. Looks like her dog, anyway."

Elle turned around. Across the room a middle-aged woman lay back in a chair with a salon attendant hovering over her. A cute little pug sat in her tote bag on the floor. Elle looked her over. Only the most fashionable women came to Pamperella, and most of them were carrying the latest jewel-covered, fur-lined designer bags. But this woman was different. Her bag was a sporty canvas tote. Hmmm, thought Elle, very interesting. And not at all the way she had imagined Nica's mother. Nica, cool, materialistic, and stylish at all costs, had a mother who carried a canvas tote bag?

"Are you sure that's her?" Elle asked.

The woman lifted her head. She looked like Nica—except for her short, dark hair—slender, pale, and attractive.

"That's her," Bibi said. "She talks about her daughter, Nica, too. How spoiled she is. How Fred gives her whatever she wants and how she'd like to take her out of boarding school and keep her at home. But her husband thinks boarding school is good for making connections or something. I don't understand people sometimes."

"You understand people too well," Elle said. "Do you think Mrs. Saunders would mind if I took Underdog over to meet her pug?"

"Not at all," Bibi said. "Just wait until your nail polish dries, if you don't mind."

Ten minutes later, her silver nail polish safely dry, Elle picked up Underdog. "Want to make a new friend?" she asked him, and took him over to Mrs. Saunders.

Her facial was done, and now Mrs. Saunders was having her hair styled. "What an adorable dog!" she said as Elle approached. "What is his name?"

"Underdog," Elle said.

Mrs. Saunders picked up her pug. "This is Juicy." She held Juicy nose to nose with Underdog and shook her slightly. "Hello! Say hello, Juicy! Hello, Underdog!"

Underdog, while indeed adorable, did not like to be treated like a baby. He gave Juicy a quick lick, then turned his face away. Juicy drooled. A lot. That must be why she's called Juicy, Elle thought.

"I'm Elle Woods," Elle said. "I know your daughter, Nica. Bibi told me you were her mother, so I wanted to introduce myself."

"How nice!" Mrs. Saunders said. "You can call me Marla. How do you know Nica?"

"We surf at Seal Beach," Elle said. "She's a great surfer."

"She should be—we've paid for enough trips to Hawaii. I'm always trying to get her to look at the beautiful Polynesian landscape, the flowers and birds, but all she wants to do is shop and surf. I haven't been to Seal Beach—is it nice?"

"It's beautiful," Elle said. "But something strange is going on there. The cove is a nesting area for seals, but they've all disappeared. Someone is driving pilings into the water at night. I think that has sent the seals away."

"That's terrible!" Marla said.

"I even found an abandoned baby seal on the beach the other day," Elle said. "Her mother never came back for her."

"Oh, my!" Marla looked stricken.

"The weird thing is, your husband's company is putting in the pilings," Elle said. "At least, the truck had his company's name on it."

Marla's expression changed from horror to suspicion. "My husband's company? At night?"

Elle nodded. She hoped she wasn't stirring up conflict in the Saunders family. But it was worth it if it helped to save Sassy's life.

Marla gave a short, brittle laugh. "He keeps telling me he's working, but I never believe him. Mostly because he won't tell me what he's working on, or where. And now I understand why. Fred is up to one of his old tricks."

"Tricks?"

Marla's expression changed again, to nervousness. She glanced around the room as if to make sure no one was listening. "I'm sorry, Elle. I can't say any more. Look, you've already spoiled your manicure. Go back to Bibi and have her fix it."

"What?" Elle studied her hands. Her manicure looked perfect. "But I—"

"Just go," Marla said. "Good luck with that poor little seal."

Elle didn't move at first. She stared at Marla, wondering what had caused her sudden change of heart.

"Go," Marla whispered.

Elle got up and returned to Bibi. "What did she say?" Bibi asked.

"Nothing, really," Elle said. "She wasn't all that helpful. She told me to go away."

"Huh," Bibi said. "That doesn't sound like Marla. She loves animals. I thought she'd do anything she could to help you try to save Sassy."

"I guess not."

"Well, come on over to the foot sink," Bibi said. "Time for your pedi. That will cheer you up."

But even having her feet rubbed and sanded smooth didn't make Elle feel better. She'd hoped Mrs. Saunders would give her the answers she needed. Now she had to find another way to get them. But she couldn't think of one.

Mrs. Saunders was gone by the time Elle returned to Bibi's regular station. Elle sat in Bibi's chair. The next procedure: touching up her highlights.

"Let's go a little lighter," Bibi said. "It's summer, after all."

"Whatever," Elle said. She picked up the magazine she'd left on the seat and opened it. Something fell out and fluttered to the floor. Elle reached down to pick it up. It was an envelope.

"What's this?" Elle said.

Bibi shrugged. "Someone must have left it in there."

Elle turned it over. Her name was scrawled on the front, in lipstick.

"It's for me," Elle said.

"Open it," Bibi said.

Elle opened the envelope. Inside was a note.

Elle read it in silence.

*I hope you'll forgive my coldness a few min-
utes ago. You must understand—I have to be
careful what I say. I am married to a very
influential man who expects me to support
him. But after I heard about Sassy, I had to
help you.*

*F.S. is a cutthroat businessman. When he
wants something, he'll do whatever he has to
to get it. That means bribing politicians,
lying to reporters, having people fired . . .*

*And he wants Seal Beach. He has already
drawn up the plans, and they're big: luxury
houses, a marina and a yacht club, a five-
star restaurant . . . He doesn't own the land
yet and doesn't have permission to build on
it. But he is sure he will get it. He regularly
bribes state senators and town councilmen.
They have been in his pocket for years. He is
sure that they will change the zoning laws
and sell the land to him on the cheap.*

*I'm afraid there's not much you can do.
But if you try, I wish you the best.*

Madame X

"What does it say?" Bibi asked.

"It's an anonymous note, but I know who it's from."

"Marla?" Bibi whispered.

Elle nodded. "She says Mr. Saunders is totally lying about his plans for Seal Beach. It's worse than I thought. He's building practically a whole town!"

"I thought that was illegal," Bibi said.

"It doesn't matter," Elle said. "He's bribing politicians to make it legal."

"Can't anyone stop him?" Bibi said.

"There's got to be a way," Elle said. "We have to tell people what's happening! Everyone in town would fight the zoning change if they knew the seals were in danger."

"Just tell them Sassy's story," Bibi said. "She's so adorable. The whole state would support you if they knew she was in trouble."

"You're right," Elle said. "I've got to reach as many people as I can, as quickly as possible. I'm going to go to the TV news station right now. I'm sure once I tell the reporters what's going on, they'll investigate and find out everything they need to know to reveal Mr. Saunders's plan."

"But what about your highlights?" Bibi said.

"I'll come back later," Elle said. "This is urgent."

"More important than touching up your high-lights?" Bibi said. "Sweetie, you'd better look in the mirror."

Elle didn't have to look in the mirror. She already knew her roots were a mess, and she didn't care. She was off to give the local TV station, KICK, the news story of the year.

Chapter 9

"I'm sorry, but we can't let you in without authorization." The receptionist at KICK TV—a skinny guy just out of college, with glasses and a crooked tie—was tougher than he looked.

"But I'm telling you, I've got a huge scoop!" she said, pouting. She stamped her freshly manicured foot. Then she tried shaking Underdog in the receptionist's face in an intimidating way, but tiny Underdog didn't scare many people. "A news flash!"

"Well, here's a news flash for you, schweetheart," the receptionist said in a Humphrey Bogart voice. "Kooks and crackpots come here every day with big stories, see?" He dropped his voice before continuing. "A lot of them have seen UFOs. Sometimes they've seen actual aliens. One guy told us that Santa and the tooth fairy had mated and created a superchild named Fairy Claus. Or was it Toothy Claus? Santa Tooth?"

"But—" Elle tried to get him to listen. "But I'm not—"

"That's why we have the KICK tips hotline," the receptionist said, ignoring her attempts to be heard, "for nuts like you. Call this number, tell us what you've got, and we'll have a reporter investigate—if it's not crazy."

"My story is nothing like that at all," Elle said. "I hope you listen to that hotline yourself, because you are going to *kick* yourself when you hear what I have to say."

"I'm kicking myself already. See?" He swiveled in his chair and showed Elle the way he was tapping one foot against the other. "Now, scram."

"You know, just because you use old-fashioned slang like 'scram' and 'crackpot,' that doesn't make you a reporter," Elle said. "Or cool."

"Thanks for the tip. See ya, Toots." The receptionist yawned, then answered his ringing telephone. "KICK News. Get a *kick* out of life," he recited in a monotone. "How can I direct your call?"

Discouraged, Elle went home and called the

KICK tips hotline. A recorded voice asked her to leave a message. She said, "My name is Elle Woods, and I want to report an environmental scandal involving greedy developers and local politicians. This is a matter of life and death! But it's too complicated to explain on an answering machine. Please call me on my cell phone as soon as you get this message. Thank you." She left her cell number and added, "I have reliable sources!" Then she hung up.

Elle sighed and looked out the window. The sky had cleared up, and the sun was shining. The house was quiet. Zosia had gone out to do errands. Bernard was napping. Elle's father was at the club playing golf, and her mother was shopping.

Since the weather had improved and her trip to the TV station had been a bust, Elle decided to go to the beach, after all. Hunter would be there, and probably Laurette. Maybe they could help her figure out a way to get this story on the news.

She and Underdog drove to the beach in her convertible, her surfboard in the back. It was a good feeling to pull up at Seal Beach in a convertible on a hot day.

Elle shaded her eyes and checked out the water. The waves were coming fast. She saw Hunter catch a big one and ride it all the way in, twisting and turning to keep one step ahead of it. He was such a great surfer. You couldn't miss him, even from a distance. He was taller and leaner than any other boy on the beach, and his black hair gleamed like sealskin in the sun. And he had his own unmistakable surfing style. Of all the surfers, including even Nica and Clive, he was the most graceful.

Elle tore herself away from watching him and went to set up her blanket and umbrella on the sand next to Laurette.

"What's new, Magoo?" Laurette asked.

"A lot," Elle said. She spilled the whole story. As she spoke, Nica walked past, obscured by Elle's umbrella. Elle didn't notice her until she saw two long, slender legs stop in front of her. One bony foot angrily kicked sand on Elle's blanket.

"What did you say to my mother?" Nica demanded, red-faced and furious. "She came home from the salon and said she'd met you. But she was all upset. She locked herself in her room and wouldn't come out."

"I'm sorry, Nica," Elle said. "I didn't do anything to upset her. Maybe she was upset about something else."

"No—you did something," Nica said. "I know you did. And after I was so nice to you the other day. Trying to help you learn to surf. What was I thinking?"

"Maybe it's your father," Elle said. "Maybe he upset her."

"How could he?" Nica said. "He's never home. Did you say something to her about those trucks you saw? Which is none of your business, by the way."

"I only told her what I told you," Elle said. "What I saw with my own eyes. A Saunders truck digging near the seal cove."

"I explained that," Nica said. "The visitors' center."

"Sorry, Nica. That doesn't make sense," Laurette said.

"I'm warning you, Elle," Nica said, her tone suddenly ominous. "If you embarrass me and my father, you'll regret it. He's a powerful man. You can't beat him."

She stalked away, kicking sand up behind her as she went.

"She has a point," Laurette said. "Even if you get the TV reporters to listen to you, you're accusing a powerful man of doing something illegal, and you have no real proof. It's your word against his. He's a well-connected businessman, and you're a sixteen-year-old, going into eleventh grade. Who do you think people will believe?"

"I don't care if he's powerful," Elle said. "He can't get away with hurting the seals. Eventually, people will believe the truth."

Chessie came running up and slid onto Elle's blanket like a batter stealing a base. "Nica's all upset!" she said. "She won't tell me why, but she said it was your fault. As if I couldn't have guessed."

"I didn't mean to upset her," Elle said. "I'm only trying to do what's right."

"Why?" Chessie said. "What's right is what makes people like you, and right now Nica doesn't like you very much. Just thought I'd tell you so you can do something to rectify the situation before it's too late."

Elle was distracted by a flyer in Chessie's hand. "What's that?" she asked.

"Nothing that concerns you," Chessie said, but she let Elle see the flyer anyway. "Sunrise has a stack of them at the shack."

The flyer said:

SURFCHIX SURF GEAR CO. PRESENTS THE FIRST ANNUAL

SURFCHIX BEACH PARTY!

At Seal Beach, Saturday, August 14
FEATURING:
Surfing Contest
Bikini Design Contest
Battle of the Bands

PLUS:
food, games, music, and much more!

Enter a contest or just hang at the beach.
The party will be broadcast on national TV!
Check our Web site for complete contest rules.

The winner of each contest will become a national
spokesperson for SurfChix, the finest in bathing suits
and surf gear for guys and, especially, girls.

"Huh," Elle said. "They're having all that right here?"

"Duh. It's one of the best surf beaches around," Chessie said. "For those in the know. And those whose so-called boyfriends are in the know. Ahem."

"Are you going to enter one of the contests?" Elle asked Chessie.

"I'm going to enter *all* of the contests," Chessie said. "Well, maybe not the Battle of the Bands, since I'm not in a band. But who knows? I really want to be the SurfChix girl. Of course, Nica will probably enter the contest, and she'll be impossible to beat, in any category."

As if to emphasize the point, Nica caught a wave and rode it cleanly while looking fabulous. Her bikini, which Elle had been too freaked out to notice earlier, was, as usual, expensive and impeccably chic.

Hunter and Brett both came out of the water dripping to sit with Elle on her blanket.

"You're going to enter the SurfChix surfing contest, right, Hunter?" Chessie said.

"The what?" Hunter looked at Elle, who passed him the flyer.

"Don't bother, man," Brett said. "I'll beat you senseless."

"You think?" Hunter said.

"No way," Chessie said. "Hunter's way better than you, Brett."

"You'd root for Hunter over your own brother?" Laurette said. "That's cold."

"Chessie!" Nica shouted from the shoreline. "What are you doing with *her*? I told you, she's our

80

mortal enemy! Get over here!"

Chessie looked anxiously from Hunter to Elle and back to Hunter again. Elle may have been her mortal enemy, but Hunter was her dreamboat. She hated to leave him all alone with Elle, even though Elle *was* his girlfriend.

"Chessie!" Nica screeched again.

"Coming!" Chessie got to her feet. "You'd better apologize to Nica or you'll be committing social suicide," she said to Elle.

"I'm willing to take that risk," Elle said.

Brett snorted. "Social suicide. Everything's a big drama with her." He wandered off.

"What's happening with Sassy?" Hunter asked Elle.

"We've got to find a way to get to the media," Elle said. "I left message on the KICK tips hotline, but somehow I have a feeling no one will take it seriously."

"No problem," Hunter said. "You're looking at the former next-door neighbor of Drea Dreiser, KICK anchorwoman. She used to babysit me."

"You're kidding!" Elle threw her arms around Hunter's neck.

Laurette laughed. "You mean, *I'm Drea Dreiser and this is KICK news. That's a kick in the head.*

Back to you, Stan. That Drea Dreiser?"

"Uh-huh," Hunter said.

"That's perfect! So you can get me in to talk to her?" Elle asked.

"Shouldn't be a problem," Hunter said. "I've got dirt on her you wouldn't believe. Her boyfriend used to sneak over while she was babysitting, all the time. I saw everything."

"Way to come through in a pinch!" Elle gave Hunter a big, happy kiss. How perfect could a guy be?

Chapter 10

"YOU'RE RIGHT, Elle," Drea Dreiser said. "If what you say is true, this could be a big story. I just wish we had more than an anonymous note to back it up."

Elle sat in Drea's dressing room at KICK TV wearing a powder blue business suit she'd bought just for the occasion. Eva said powder blue was the new power-suit color. And anyway, it made Elle's big blue eyes stand out more than ever. "Bat your eyelashes a few times, and who could resist you?" Zosia said.

Whatever Elle had done, it seemed to be working.

Elle was dismayed, however, when Drea asked if they could talk while a guy named Benny hovered around her doing her hair and makeup for the six o'clock broadcast. Elle thought Drea wasn't taking her seriously; she wouldn't talk to an *adult* from the makeup chair, would she?

And in fact, Drea *was* somewhat skeptical and condescending toward Elle at first. After all, Elle was little Hunter Perry's girlfriend. Drea had known Hunter when he was a sweet kid who couldn't sleep without his teddy bear.

But as she listened to the story of Sassy and the mysterious nightly construction, Drea's expression grew more and more serious.

"I'll put a reporter on the story right away," Drea said. "We'll interview state officials and Fred Saunders himself. Maybe some of his employees, too. That'll give the story more credibility. We'll get to the bottom of this. You'll probably see something on the air in the next few days."

"Excellent!" Elle said. "Thank you!"

"You're welcome," Drea said. "Here at KICK we live to serve. Benny, you're putting on too much mascara again! I told you, lighten up with the wand!"

"Sorry, Drea." Benny quickly blotted away the excess mascara. He seemed a little frightened of Drea.

"How's Hunter, by the way?" Drea asked,

switching moods so abruptly that Elle was taken aback. "He was such a cute little boy. I bet he's good-looking now, isn't he?"

"He is," Elle said. "And he remembers *you* very well, too. And your boyfriend, Gary."

Drea's color drained under the pancake makeup.

Benny grinned. "Guess I know who to talk to if I ever need to blackmail you, huh, Drea?" he joked.

"Hunter doesn't remember anything," Drea said. "He was too young."

Elle didn't say any more. She didn't want to make Drea so mad she wouldn't help. But she was glad she'd helped to make Benny feel less nervous.

"Elle, I have an idea," Drea said, shouting, "Crystal! Get in here!"

Drea's assistant, Crystal, ran into the dressing room, looking frazzled.

"Crystal, this is Elle Woods. Take her into the studio and have one of the cameramen shoot a brief statement from her. Get a producer to supervise it." Drea turned to Elle. "Go make your statement on camera. We'll use it in the story. Just tell the producer what you saw and what you believe is happening. Okay?"

Elle was delighted. "Perfect! Thanks!"

Drea stood up, the paper makeup smock still

wrapped around her neck, and offered Elle her hand. "Nice to meet you, and thanks for the tip."

Elle followed Crystal into the studio, walking on air. Now Mr. Saunders was in for it. Once everyone found out what he was up to, he'd have to stop building on Seal Beach.

For the next few days, Elle obsessively watched KICK news, waiting for her story to air. She watched the morning show, the noontime news, the five o'clock, six o'clock, eleven o'clock, and late-night updates.

"It's a good thing school's out," Laurette said. "So you have plenty of time for TV. You don't need little inconveniences like classes and homework eating up all your time."

"Where is my story?" Elle asked, ignoring Laurette's sarcasm. They were at Laurette's house, waiting for the five o'clock news. "What's taking them so long to put it on the air?"

"I guess it takes time to do the legwork," Laurette said. "The research, the interviews. The long lag time probably means the story will be thorough." The news came on, and the anchors introduced themselves.

"I'm Stan Gomez."

"And I'm Drea Dreiser." Drea announced, "Tonight, a heartwarming story of one man's quest to save a seal colony. But first: what is the one scent that can help *you* seem five to ten years younger? We'll have the answer when we come back in sixty seconds."

Elle was confused. "One man's quest to *save* a seal colony? What are they talking about?"

Laurette shrugged. "Maybe they found a man who wants to stop Mr. Saunders."

"I hope so," Elle said.

The news came back from commercial. Elle sat impatiently through the story about the exciting discovery of the scent that made one seem younger (grapefruit). Frankly, seeming younger was the last thing she was worried about just then.

"And now," Drea said, "meet Frank Saunders. He's a local developer who usually builds on a very big scale." Video of Frank Saunders, smiling like a jolly, ruddy Santa Claus as he walked along the shore, was playing. "But a little seal pup named Sassy won his heart." There was an adorable shot of Sassy in her pool at the wildlife refuge. "And now he's putting aside business to make something very small . . . for Sassy." Frank sat beside Sassy, patting her on the head while she hopped up and down.

"What?" Elle couldn't understand what she was seeing and hearing on the screen. Was she dreaming? Hallucinating?

"Saunders is building a small recreation area on Seal Beach, near the site of a former seal nesting area," said Drea. "The area will include a dock and a visitors' center, all built according to the most ecologically sound principles, to raise money to help protect these endangered animals. And he's setting aside a special cove just for the seals." The video showed the seal rookery and the surrounding beach. It was high tide—no sign of the pilings Saunders had already installed under the water.

"I don't believe this." Elle squeezed her eyes shut and opened them again, but the picture stayed the same. "Laurette, pinch me," Elle said. "I need to return to reality!"

"I don't have the strength," Laurette said in a zombie voice. "I'm too stunned."

"This area was dangerous for seals," Frank Saunders said on camera. "And here's the proof: little Sassy. She was abandoned on Seal Beach by her mother and had to be rescued by the heroic California Park Service. The protected area we want to build will be safe for the seals. They'll come back, and people can come here and visit them and see them playing on the beach. It's whole-some, educational fun for the whole family! And good for our mother earth."

"Is he crazy?" Elle asked. "He's crazy!"

"But don't you worry that the presence of humans might scare the seals away?" Drea asked.

"Good question!" Elle shouted at the TV.

"That's a common fallacy, Drea," Frank said. "Scientists have repeatedly shown that seals actu-ally like the smell of the hot dogs and hamburgers we'll be feeding our human guests. And the hum of motorboats and soft-ice-cream machines is soothing to them. It drowns out the sound of the ocean and helps the mother seals rock their babies to sleep."

"This man has completely lost it," Laurette said. "He must think we're all morons! Who would buy all of this?"

"I don't know," Elle said. She felt as if she were trapped in a nightmare. How had everything gotten twisted around this way? "Where's the statement I taped at the station? Where's my side of the story?"

"Not everyone agrees with Saunders's plan, however," Drea said.

"Here we go," Laurette said.

"Finally," Elle said.

"We first stumbled across this story when a disgruntled Seal Beach surfer came to our studios to report that Saunders Development Company workers were doing something on the beach at night."

The scene cut to Elle, sitting in the studio in her powder blue suit.

"Wow," Laurette said. "When you wear that color your eyes really pop off the screen."

"Shhh!"

"I saw a Saunders truck working late at night near the seal cove," Elle said on TV. "It was very disturbing. I was with some friends. We were having a bonfire on the beach."

Drea's voice said, "What bothered you about it?"

"There were these bright lights," Elle said on TV. "And the truck was so noisy."

"Elle, did you say that?" Laurette said.

"No!" Elle cried. "I mean, not that way. They cut out most of what I said. And they put it in a different order! And Drea never asked me that question—she wasn't even there when I taped my statement. They made it sound like all I care about is that our bonfire was disturbed!"

"Mr. Saunders," Drea said, "why are you working at night? And what do you say to the critics who want to keep the beach to themselves?"

"I don't want to keep the beach to myself!" Elle shrieked. This was wrong, all wrong!

"We were working at night because we're modest," Saunders said. "We didn't want people to make a big fuss. This is for the seals, not for our company's reputation. But you caught us, heh-heh—" He shrugged jovially.

"And the critics?"

Mr. Saunders's face turned grave. "I don't like to see people making big statements when they don't know what they're talking about. It can be very dangerous. I'm afraid that young woman is just another blonde beach bunny who only cares about surfing and prancing around in her bikini. She seems to care more about her precious bonfire than the fate of a little seal. If people like her ran the world, the environment would be in big trouble."

"No-o-o-o-o-o!" Elle screamed. She pounded her fists on the floor. "No! No! No!"

"And there you have it," Drea said. "Proof that sometimes a big, powerful man can find room in his heart to help the small and adorable." Another shot of Frank and Sassy. The camera zoomed in on Sassy's cute face for extra effect. "I'm Drea Dreiser. Coming up next: how drinking diet soda can make you rich. We'll be back in sixty seconds."

"Laurette, have you found the energy to pinch me yet?" Elle asked. "Because I really need to wake up from this nightmare."

Laurette lightly pinched Elle's cheek. "Did that help?"

"No." Elle collapsed on the floor in despair. "What just happened? I don't understand. Frank Saunders's project drove the seals away! *He* orphaned Sassy! And now he's claiming he wants to save her? He's using her to get the public on his side, so he can change the zoning and get permission to build on the beach."

"He practically said it was all your fault," Laurette pointed out. "The guy's got major nerve."

"Once he builds the marina, it's just a small step to approving houses, stores, whatever he wants," Elle said. "The seals may never come back—but by then people will have forgotten all about them. It's diabolical."

"No seals will nest and mate so close to a working marina and a bustling tourist center," Laurette said. "I don't care what Mr. Saunders says—the roar of a motorboat is not a soothing hum. Why did Drea fall for his ridiculous story? It's full of holes."

"I don't know. I guess it's like you said: my

word against Mr. Saunders's. He's a rich, powerful grown-up. And I'm a 'blonde beach bunny.' Even in my power suit. How can I beat him? I can't win."

"Want me to pinch you again?" Laurette asked.

"No, thanks."

They lay on the floor in stunned, miserable silence. Elle felt overwhelmed. She was working all alone against a giant machine that didn't really care about anyone or anything except money. Certainly not the truth.

"Elle, you can't give up," Laurette said at last. "You may be a blonde beach bunny, but you're not dumb. And don't forget Sassy. No matter what he says, I know in my heart Mr. Saunders is not going to do a thing to bring her mother back."

"You're right," Elle said. "We can't give up—for Sassy's sake we can't. I'll show Mr. Saunders I'm not just a blonde beach bunny." Then she was quiet again, because she didn't know what to do next.

Chapter 11

SITTING ON the beach the day after the dreadful news broadcast, Elle was still stunned. She had been afraid to sleep that night, worried she'd see Mr. Saunders's arrogant face in her dreams. At breakfast, Eva had seen how worked up she was and advised her to go to the beach.

"My yoga teacher says the ocean helps relax your mind," Eva said. "The sounds of the beach help lull you into a state of not thinking. And not thinking can bring up the answers you need from your subconscious."

It sounded good. But Eva's yoga teacher hadn't counted on Chessie's voice being one of the sounds of the beach.

"I saw you on the news with Nica's father yesterday, Elle," said Chessie. "You were great! Really. Your suit was so pretty. Was it Versace? I thought I saw one like it at Barneys."

"It was Chanel," Elle said.

"Of course. How could I be so stupid? I bet you spent a lot of time shopping for just the right suit to wear on TV. The effort really showed."

"Actually, I wasn't planning on—"

"And wasn't Mr. Saunders great?" Chessie said. "He was so sweet with that seal you found. I bet you're so glad he's going to help her!"

Elle started grinding her teeth. Laurette must have heard the noise, because she cut in. "Chessie, you're giving Elle a headache. Could you leave us alone?"

"Sure. You have a headache, Elle? Poor thing! Probably from falling and bumping your head on your surfboard so much. Have you been to the doctor?"

"Chessie—" Laurette warned.

Nica came prancing up. "If it isn't Miss Beach Bunny. I told you my father would never hurt the seals. I just want to thank you for going to the news with your whole bonfire story so he could show everybody what an animal lover he is, no matter what you—or my mother—say. Now his wildlife visitors' center is sure to be approved—and it's all thanks to you."

"Elle has a headache," Chessie told her, "otherwise I'm sure she'd be jumping up and down for joy."

"*Uhnn . . .*" Elle couldn't even speak. This was too much for her.

Laurette stepped in again to defend her. "Why don't you two just get out of here and leave Elle alone?" she said. "Chessie, I think the waves are calling to you. 'Chessie Morton! We're bored! Come in and let us knock you around!'"

"Let's go, Chessie," Nica said.

"God, you'd think they'd be happy your dad is saving their stupid seal," Chessie said as they walked away.

"I can't take it," Elle said. "We've got to stop Mr. Saunders's project. He's lying. All we have to do is prove it."

"But how?" Laurette said. "What can we do? The press won't listen to you anymore—that story's over."

Plus, as Elle knew and as Laurette was nice enough not to say out loud, Mr. Saunders had painted her as an idiot. If no one had taken her seriously before, people definitely wouldn't listen to her now.

Elle lathered on sunscreen and lay back down on her towel. "Relax your brain, Laurette. Something will come to us. It has to." She closed her eyes.

"I don't really buy that yoga stuff," Laurette said. But she lay down beside Elle and closed her eyes, too.

"Try it anyway," Elle said. "My mother claims she decorated our house this way. Every time she hit a snag, she'd just relax her mind, and the answer to her problem would appear in a vision."

"Is that why she has purple velvet drapes in the guest bathroom?" Laurette asked.

"Yep."

"I see," Laurette said. "I'm still skeptical. This problem is a lot more complicated than choosing a color scheme."

"Choosing a color scheme can be pretty complicated if you let it," Elle said.

"Let's stop talking about decorating now," Laurette said.

"Okay," Elle said. "We'll just be quiet and let our minds work."

Elle could hear the waves breaking on the

shore, and the laughter and shouts of the surfers, and herself breathing, and Underdog panting beside her. Something was missing.

Hunter was out on the lineup; she'd seen him when she arrived and waved to him. That wasn't it. Still, Elle felt a hole in her beach universe.

Aha. "Where's Darren today?" she asked.

"With his band, where else?" Laurette said. "They're practicing extra hard now. They're entering the SurfChix Battle of the Bands contest. I'll probably never see him again until it's over."

"They're not a surf band," Elle said. "Why do they care about the contest so much?"

"The exposure," Laurette said. "Darren can't resist it. He's drawn to any shot at playing his music to more people. They're going to show the Battle of the Bands on TV, so just by entering, the Factor will be seen all over the country. But he wants to win."

"What does the winner get?" Elle asked.

"They'll be, like, the house band for SurfChix. They'll play on SurfChix commercials, and the company will even sponsor a tour. It's a pretty big deal. But I don't see how they'll ever win. Bands are coming from all over the world for this chance."

Elle felt the sun warm and relax her while all

this sank in. The SurfChix contest. A sponsored tour. National exposure. Your face on TV.

"Of course! That's it!" She sat straight up and poked Laurette in the ribs.

"Hey, no poking," Laurette said. "What's 'it'?"

"The SurfChix contest," Elle said. "I'll enter it, and if I win I can spread the word about saving the seals. People will have to listen to me then."

"But you're not in a band," Laurette said. "You don't even play an instrument."

"I played the recorder in third grade," Elle said.

Laurette didn't dignify that with an answer.

"It doesn't matter," Elle said. "I'll enter a different part of the contest. Where are those flyers?"

She ran over to the Sunrise Surf Shack, snagged a flyer, and hurried back. "Look—there's a surfing contest."

Laurette sat up and rested on her elbows, blinking at Elle in the sunlight. "The surfing contest? How could you win that? You've only been surfing for a couple of weeks or so, and you've never managed to make it all the way to shore—or even close."

"Thanks for the vote of confidence," Elle said. "Okay, you're right. Chances of winning the surfing contest—zero. But what about this? Bikini design. I can do that!"

Laurette snatched the flyer away and read it before handing it back. "Bikini design. You sure can do that. It's right up your alley."

"And if I win, I'll have a platform on national TV," Elle said. "I'll tell everyone about Sassy and Mr. Saunders and what he's really up to. And maybe we can stop him."

"Maybe," Laurette said. "But first you have to win."

"Oh, I'll win," Elle said, her confidence growing. "It's my destiny. I feel as if my whole life has been leading up to this moment. The homemade Barbie clothes. The handmade jewelry. The endless redecoration of my room. Now I know it all had a purpose—to win this bikini-design contest."

"Your life has meaning," Laurette said.

"That's right," Elle said. "Now, it's time to get to work."

Chapter 12

"so MY little beach bunny is going to become Queen of Bikini Design," Hunter said. He put his arm around Elle, and she nestled against him. They were sitting in a booth across from Darren and Laurette at Petronio's, a local pizza shop, waiting for their brick-oven pie.

"And my basketball star is going to be a surf god," Elle said.

"If I'm lucky," Hunter said. "I've got to beat Clive. And Nica. And who knows who else?"

"Nica's entering the surfing contest?" Elle said. Of course she was. She had a chance of winning, too.

"*And* the bikini contest," Laurette said. "So you'll have to beat her, too, Elle."

Elle groaned. "How do you know?"

"Sunrise told me she overheard Nica and Chessie talking about it. Nica said her father wants her to win at least one contest so she can become Miss SurfChix and promote his Seal Beach project."

"That's low," Hunter said.

"Nica could be tough competition," Elle said. "She has great clothes. Do you think she makes them herself?"

"No, but she probably picks them out herself," Laurette said. "She has good fashion sense. But she's not as creative as you, Elle."

"What about Chessie?" Elle asked.

"She'll never win the surf contest, that's for sure," Darren said.

"Nica and Chessie are both entering both contests," Laurette said. "I wouldn't be surprised if Nica went for the Battle of the Bands, too."

"With Chessie singing backup," Hunter said.

"No way, that's my territory," Darren said. "Warp Factor Five is going to blow the competition away."

"Have you been learning to play surf guitar?" Laurette asked.

"Not really," Darren said. "We're more indie-monster-rock types."

"But the contest is only for surf music." Elle dug

the flyer out of her bag and showed it to Darren. He took it and groaned, rubbing his head and messing up his already messy dark blond hair.

"Dude, I didn't read the fine print," he said. "I *don't* know how to play surf guitar! You ever hear how Dick Dale plays? It's, like, really fast fingering. That stuff is hard."

"I know," Elle said. "I've watched how Laurette does it. Her fingers fly over those strings."

Darren stared at Laurette. "I know you've been taking lessons but . . . you can't really play surf guitar, can you?"

"Well, I'm still learning, but that's what Sunrise has been teaching me," Laurette said. "What else would I learn to play at the beach?"

"Show me," Darren said. He got up from the table and looked around. "There's got to be a guitar around here somewhere. Everybody and his brother's in a band these days. Aha." He spotted a girl with a guitar case waiting for takeout and made a beeline for her.

"Oh, my God," Laurette said. "What's he doing?"

"Don't worry, you'll show him how good you are and blow his mind," Elle said.

"But I'm not that good yet!" Laurette said. "What if he thinks I stink?"

"He won't," Elle said. "And anyway, he needs you."

Darren dragged the girl to their table. "Laurette, this is Julie. She's been kind enough to lend you her guitar." Julie looked wary, and didn't make any move to let go of her guitar. Darren held on to her sleeve in case she tried to escape. "Just for two seconds, I swear."

"All right," Julie said. She unzipped her guitar case and passed the guitar to Laurette. "Be careful with it. It's an original Washburn, from '75."

"It's beautiful." Laurette ran her hands over the guitar and placed it in her lap.

"Okay, girl," Darren said. "Show us what you got."

Laurette started picking, tentatively at first, but then warming to it. She picked and strummed "Wipeout," a classic 1960s surf tune. She was a natural.

Everyone clapped when she was finished. She gave the guitar back to Julie and thanked her.

"You sounded great," Julie said. "How long have you been playing?"

"A few weeks," Laurette said.

"Amazing," Julie said. "If you ever want to jam, give me a call." She scribbled her name and number on a piece of paper and handed it to Laurette.

"Sometimes we need an extra guitar player."

"Thanks." Laurette put the paper with the number on it into her bag, and Julie went off to pick up her pizza.

Darren fell to his knees. "Laurette, dudette, you have to be in my band," he pleaded. Laurette grinned.

"I don't know," she said. "I'm not sure I want to mix love and the rawk. You know what they say—nothing ruins good music like a guy always hanging around. A male Yoko. Maybe I'd have more fun playing with Julie."

"No! Laurette, I was so wrong," Darren said. "The thing about Yoko was, she didn't jibe with the Beatles' music. But you—you'd jibe perfectly with us! Please, Laurette. I'll never learn those Dick Dale riffs in time."

Laurette looked at Elle, milking the situation for all it was worth. "What do you think, Elle?"

"It would be a step down for you," Elle said, teasingly. "But after all, Darren is your boyfriend. Maybe you should help him out."

"Would you two stop torturing the poor guy and just say yes?" Hunter said. "You know you want to do it, Laurette. You've been saying so all summer."

Laurette laughed. "Okay, Darren. Yes. I'd love to play with Warp Factor Five."

"All right," Darren said. "Next rehearsal is tomorrow at two, Mike's garage. We've got this battle nailed."

Elle nudged Laurette under the table. "Yay! You're a rock chick!"

"Maybe I'll write a song about Sassy and Mr. Saunders," Laurette said. "I'll call it 'Mr. Saunders Lies.'"

"Hold on," Darren said. "No message songs. Band rules."

"What if I feel like breaking the rules, just this once?" Laurette said.

"Seriously, Darren. Think about how guilty you'd feel if Sassy never saw her mother again," Elle said, "and it was all because *your band* had a rule against message songs."

Darren messed his hair some more. "You girls really know how to twist the knife. All right, write whatever you want. I don't promise we'll play it, but we'll see."

Laurette kissed him. "Thanks. I'll stop making demands now—for a little while."

"You're turning out to be a great boyfriend, Darren," Elle said.

"Against all early predictions," Laurette joked.

Darren blushed and looked away. He was shy about the whole boyfriend thing.

"Hey, what about me?" Hunter said.

"You've always been the best," Elle said. "And I knew you would be from the first day I laid eyes on you."

Their pizza arrived. Each couple kissed. Then they all dug in.

Chapter 13

ELLE SPENT the next evening in her room dreaming up the perfect bikini. What would her ideal suit be? She sketched a few ideas. It should be pink, because pink was her favorite color. A nice, bright pink, so a girl could be seen from the beach as she rode the waves. But what else?

It should look good on everybody, Elle thought. And it should be fashionable and cute and never ride up or fall down, no matter what its wearer was doing.

But how would she accomplish all that? Even professional swimsuit designers hadn't managed to make a suit that stayed on perfectly, as far as Elle could tell, and she'd tried on a *lot* of suits. Maybe it was impossible. But Elle wouldn't accept that until she knew it for sure, firsthand.

There was nothing else to do but get started. She drew a few sketches, then made a tiny pattern. Her first model would be Underdog. Elle figured he'd be easy to work with. And plus, he was the only model available to her twenty-four hours a day.

"You looked so pretty on the news last week," Bibi said as she brushed out Elle's long hair in preparation for the highlights, "and very businesslike. Did you know powder blue was the new power-suit color?"

"That's what I heard. Did you notice my roots?" Elle asked. She flipped through a fashion magazine, looking for pictures of bathing suits. She had a stack of magazines at home, but she'd found one at the salon that she hadn't seen yet.

"*I* noticed them, but I'm sure no one else did," Bibi said. "I only saw them because I knew they were there."

"I noticed them, too," Elle said. "Roots are definitely not the most important thing on my mind right now, but I'm desperate to win that contest. We have to model our bikinis ourselves—and perform some kind of activity in them, to show how they work as activewear. I've got to look my best."

"Say no more. One headful of fabulous sun-kissed highlights, coming up," Bibi said.

"What do you think of this bikini?" Elle showed her a picture of a model in a bra and boy shorts with orange-and-black stripes.

"Eh, I'm not crazy about horizontal stripes," Bibi said. "It looks like a Halloween costume. And black nail polish on the beach? Ew."

Elle turned the page. "What about this one?" The picture showed a deeply tanned girl in a white string bikini with a thong bottom.

"That's tiny," Bibi said. "I don't think a surf gear company would pick a thong. But at least her nails look good. See how that pale polish complements her complexion? I'd recommend pale pink nail polish—or maybe bronze—to show off your tan. When you get one."

"I'm working on it," Elle said. Zosia was constantly warning her about the aging effects of the sun on her skin. Elle wouldn't see those effects for years, but Zosia knew how to paint a scary picture, which she illustrated with photos of her wrinkled relatives in Poland.

"They just can't stay away from the Baltic Sea," Zosia clucked. She waved a photo of a particularly grizzled old lady whose skin looked like the skin on an elephant's foot. "This is my Aunt Janina. Do you know how old she was when this picture was taken? Thirty-seven!"

Elle shuddered, and from then on, she followed Zosia's advice: always wear sunscreen and a hat. But that had kept her looking pasty white. She still didn't have the California-beach-girl look down. But she had a plan to remedy that.

"I've decided to go with a spray-on tan," she told Bibi.

"Good idea," Bibi said, "You could use a little color. Makes any bikini look better." She paused to give Underdog a treat. He was snuggled inside the large tote bag Elle carried him in, half hidden. "What's the latest on Sassy?"

"I took Underdog to the wildlife refuge to visit her yesterday," Elle said. "He loves her so much. It's too bad she's too young for him."

"And there is the little problem of their being completely different species," Bibi said.

"Yes, that, too," Elle said. She sighed, remembering the visit. Sassy's eyes had lost some of their sparkle, and she wasn't as playful as a growing seal pup should be. Even Underdog seemed to sense that something was wrong. Once they got home, he had spent the rest of the day moping in his velvet bed.

"Sassy's not doing well," Elle told Bibi. "She's not eating as much as she should, and not growing as fast as she ought to. The ranger said a baby seal really needs her mother."

Bibi shook her head. "That is so sad. Elle, you've got to win this contest so you can get word of Sassy's plight to the people."

"I've already started working on it," Elle said. Underdog sat happily inside the tote bag, munching on his treat. Elle reached in, pulled him out, and set him on her lap. He was wearing a pink-and-yellow flowered bandeau around his chest and what looked like a matching diaper.

"Ta-da! What do you think?"

Bibi looked at Underdog and plucked the fabric of his bikini. "I don't know, Elle. The material's kind of bunchy on the bottom. But maybe that's because you're using a dog as a mannequin."

"No, you're right," Elle said. "It's hard to make perfect-fitting bottoms. My prototypes keep bunching!"

"You know how hard it is just to *find* the perfect swimsuit," Bibi said. "Imagine how hard it must be to make one." She paused to paint dye on a strand of Elle's hair and wrap it in foil. "You know, I saw Marla Saunders the other day. She's so upset about how her husband twisted your story around that she was going to retreat to a spa in Arizona. She didn't know how long she'd stay there. She said she was so mad she couldn't speak to her husband and couldn't stand the sight of his face. And Nica made her angry, too, taking her father's side the way she did."

"Nica's entering the SurfChix contest," Elle said. "Bikini design and surfing. Because her father wants her to be the spokesmodel for his development. Can you believe that?"

"I can," Bibi said. "You've got to beat her, Elle, and make sure your boyfriend or somebody beats her at surfing."

"I'll do my best," Elle said.

"Drop your chin a little," Bibi said. Elle tilted her head forward, and Bibi applied more highlights. "Listen, I'll put you in touch with a friend of mine. She's a swimwear model. Maybe she could give you some design tips or hook you up with a fashion show or photo shoot or something. Her name's Carina."

"Carina what?"

"Just Carina. She's a one-namer."

"Thanks, Bibi," Elle said. "That would help a lot. I thought I could figure out how to design a bathing suit. But I'm realizing I don't know the first thing about it. It's much harder than it looks."

Bibi glanced at Underdog in his tiny prototype bikini. "Yes, I can see that."

Elle met Carina at a studio where she and some other models were doing a magazine shoot. Carina, a lanky brunette, was wearing a terry-cloth bathrobe. She led Elle to the models' dressing room.

"Thanks so much for meeting me," Elle said.

"Anything for Bibi," Carina said. "I adore her."

"Me, too." Elle shifted her tote to make sure Underdog had enough air. He was dressed in her latest creation, a gingham bathing suit decorated with fuzzy little bumblebee appliqués.

"A dog in a bikini!" Carina said. "That's cute. What's her name?"

"It's a he. His name is Underdog."

"Why is he wearing a bikini? Is he gay?"

"No, he's just a good sport."

Carina looked a little confused. "Oh." She sat down in a chair while a makeup artist went to work on her face. Elle felt as if she'd watched a lot of people having their makeup done lately.

"Meet Juanita, Marina, and Tina." Carina introduced three other models: a black girl with very short hair; a cat-eyed blonde; and an Asian girl with long, dark hair. "And these are the suits we'll be wearing today. They're all by Zola Plunkett. She's my favorite designer. Take a look at them if you like."

Elle scanned the long row of bathing suits hanging on a garment rack. "I guess you've all worn a lot of bikinis in your careers, right?" Elle asked.

"Totally," Juanita said.

"So what kind do you like best?" Elle asked.

"Best in what way?" Marina asked.

"Well, what kind is the most comfortable?" Elle said.

"I really don't care about comfort," Tina said. "I just want to look good."

"Okay, which kind looks best on you?"

"I like those one-piece suits with the cutouts on the tummy," Marina said.

"They're cool," Elle said. "But they're not bikinis. The contest is for bikinis only."

"In that case, the tinier the better," Tina said. "I think I look best naked, so I like to wear as little as possible."

Elle tried not to make a face. This wasn't very

helpful so far. Most people didn't feel as comfortable naked as Tina seemed to. Elle already knew she didn't want to make a super-tiny suit, because it wouldn't be good to surf in. And there was no way she was modeling a thong in front of a huge crowd of people.

"I agree with Tina," Juanita said. "I hate those practical suits that cover up your bottom. They just scream, 'Mommy.'"

Carina laughed. "I actually call them Mommy suits."

"But that's because you're models," Elle said. "Some people don't want their bodies hanging out all over the place."

"That's not our problem, is it?" Marina said.

"I guess not," Elle said. "What about keeping your suit in place? Even if you're wearing a teeny bikini, you still don't want it to slip, do you?"

"I do," Carina said. "It's sexy." She demonstrated by peeling off the strap of her bra top and letting it hang down her arm. She pushed her bare shoulder forward and pursed her lips to give Elle the full effect.

"It is sexy," Elle said. "But I need to make something more practical. Don't you have any tricks for, say, keeping your straps from falling down when you dive into the water?"

"The photographer usually likes it when they fall down," Tina said, and they all giggled.

"But what *if*, and I'm just saying if, you're by yourself, not having your picture taken, at a pool party," Elle said. "Don't you worry about your suit slipping when you go off the diving board?"

All four models looked puzzled. "If something slips, I just fix it," Juanita said. "But frankly, I'm not the diving-board type."

"Me, either," Marina said.

"I like to dive naked," Tina said.

"All right, how about this," Elle said. "Let's say you were judging a contest for best bikini. Which one of these would you pick?"

The models scanned the samples they were about to put on. After a few minutes, Carina pointed to a hot-pink bikini with a flower at the hip and at the back of the neck, where the halter top tied.

"The pink one," she said.

"The pink one," Juanita said.

Tina nodded and Marina said, "Definitely the pink one."

"Okay," Elle said. "Now we're getting somewhere." This confirmed her instinct to go with pink. The flower at the hip would get in the way of surfing, but the flower at the back of the neck was cute and different.

"Oh, and Elle?" Carina said. "I'd advise you not to put any padding in the bra. I hate that."

"I hate that, too," Juanita said. "It doesn't dry as fast as the rest of the suit."

Elle jotted down the words *No padding in bra*. "Thank you all. You've been very helpful."

"Wait—one more thing," Tina said. "Those high-cut legs? They're not very flattering on people with big thighs. Not that I'd know. But I've seen it around. Yecchhh."

"Got it. No high-cut legs. Anything else?"

Once they got started, the models couldn't stop. Ideas kept occurring to them, and they gave Elle suggestions throughout the whole photo shoot. Some—like a preference for see-through crochet— were less helpful than others.

"I still say naked is best," Tina said.

Chapter 14

"LAURETTE, SHE'S doing it again." Elle could hear Eva's voice outside the door of her room. "You'd think she had exams to study for or something, the way she's been acting. She won't let anyone in except for Bernard, and all he's allowed to do is bring her sandwiches and take the empty plates away."

"There's nothing to worry about," Elle heard Laurette reply. "It's just like her basketball and cheerleading obsessions. It will pass." There was a knock on the door, and Elle knew it was Laurette and not her mother, because it was more a tap than a desperate banging.

"Come in," Elle said.

"It's always so easy for you," Eva said to Laurette in the hall outside. "She just lets you right in. Why won't she be that way with me?"

"Maybe because you're too nosy," Elle said. "Now, go away, please."

Laurette shut the door behind her. Elle was in the middle of watching a Gidget DVD. Laurette looked at the screen and shook her head. Elle was definitely in the zone.

Elle had been locked inside all morning, sketching bikini ideas while gorging on beach movies. *Beach Blanket Bingo* and *Muscle Beach Party*, starring Annette Funicello and Frankie Avalon, were funny for the outdated slang. But as far as bikinis went, those early-sixties suits were as big and over-constructed as Annette's beehive hairdo. The bottoms looked like girdles or, worse, diapers. And the torpedo-bra tops would never fly today. Talk about padding!

Elle loved the Gidget movies, and noted a few ideas for fabric patterns and cute details from Gidget's bikinis. But her favorite movie was *Blue Crush*, because it was all about surfer girls. Elle couldn't believe their moves. If only she could surf like that.

The *Blue Crush* girls surfed in all kinds of little

bikinis. But Elle noticed that during the big competition, when it counted, they wore rash guards—nylon-and-Lycra tops meant to be worn under a wet suit. Elle liked the look of them, but they were definitely not bikinis. Sometimes the girls in the movie surfed in board shorts, which also cut out a lot of the slippage problems. Shorts were practical and cute, but they weren't bikinis, either. And they tended to sag unappealingly when wet.

"Any brilliant inspirations?" Laurette asked.

"Not really," Elle said. "I need to come up with something different, you know? Something that will make the judges say, 'Wow!' And all this is old news."

Underdog strutted past in Elle's latest attempt at a prototype: a combo bullet bra and teeny G-string.

"What the heck is that?" Laurette asked.

"I call it the Marilyn Gisele," Elle said. "I was trying to combine old-fashioned 1960s voluptuousness with up-to-date Brazilian sexiness."

"Sorry, but it's just not working." Laurette picked up Underdog and petted him. "Poor boy. What is Elle putting you through?"

"He's starting to get impatient. I'm not sure how many more prototypes he'll sit still for." She gave Laurette a meaningful stare. "Maybe it's time to replace him with another model."

A look of horror flashed across Laurette's face. She dropped Underdog on the bed. "Don't look at me. I'm no swimsuit model."

"I just need a body to try things on," Elle said, "so I can see what the bikinis look like and how they move."

"What about Zosia?" Laurette said. "Don't your parents pay her to do things like that?"

"They don't pay her to model," Elle said, "but she might be willing to do it, anyway. Did you know she was once Miss Gdańsk?"

"Really? I'm not surprised," Laurette said. "So she's used to walking around half-naked in front of millions of people. She'd be a much better model than I would."

"She's too opinionated," Elle said. "She'd nag me about every little detail, and I wouldn't be able to think."

"What about me?" Laurette looked offended. "Are you saying I'm not opinionated?"

"Not about bikinis," Elle said. "Not so much."

"Granted," Laurette said. "When are you breaking out of this prison? Want to hit the beach with me? I've been cooped up in Mike's garage practicing all morning and I need some fresh air." She pointed Elle's face in the direction of the mirror. "And so do you. You're looking paler than ever."

"But . . . the movies . . . I haven't watched them all yet."

"They can wait," Laurette said. "Let's book."

"Paddle! Paddle!" Hunter shouted. He pushed Elle's surfboard toward the shore as a nice, modest wave rolled up behind them. Elle paddled hard, but then she thought she felt something snap on her bikini top. She stopped paddling and missed the wave.

"Aw, Elle, you could have gotten that one," Hunter said. Elle paddled back to where he floated in the lineup.

"I thought my strap broke," Elle said. "I felt *something.*"

"Forget about your straps," Hunter said. "Concentrate! The waves are perfect for you today, nice and easy. Now turn around. Let's get this next one."

He turned Elle's board around to face the shore. He waited until the right moment, then pushed her once again and shouted, "Go!"

She paddled and paddled. This time she wasn't going to let anything distract her, not the two pieces of Lycra covering her top, not the one piece covering her bottom, not her hair getting into her eyes or the other surfers in her way—nothing. She paddled hard, caught the front edge of the wave, and stepped up on her board.

"Woo-hoo!" she heard Hunter call behind her. "You're doing it! Go, Elle, go!"

But apparently, something *had* snapped on her last ride, because she suddenly noticed that the straps that tied her bikini top behind her back were hanging down—and her top was flying loose! She grabbed the straps with both hands. The wave pitched her board into the air. Wipeout!

"Stupid top!" she muttered as the wave crashed over her head.

"Elle, you had it!" Hunter swam up to her and helped her catch her board. "What happened?"

"My top came off," Elle said.

"So you lost your concentration," Hunter said.

"What was I supposed to do?" Elle said. "Let it go?"

"I guess not," Hunter said. "This keeps happening to you. You need a better bathing suit."

"Tell me about it," Elle said. She swam in to shore to rest for a few minutes.

"Hey, Elle, thanks for the peep show!" Nica teased.

"I really respect the way you're so comfortable with your body," Chessie said, "and nudity and all."

Nica cracked up. Underdog left his spot under the beach umbrella and ran up to Elle, barking happily at the sight of her. He was wearing Elle's latest prototype, a cropped tankini.

"Oh . . . my . . . God," Nica said. "What is that? What is he wearing?"

"It's a cropped tankini top with boy shorts," Elle said. "I was just testing it out as an idea."

"That's not your entry for the contest, is it?" Chessie said. "I mean, it looks so cute on him. It's the perfect bathing suit—for a dog."

"And a boy dog at that," Nica said. "Is Underdog going to be your model?" They laughed.

"Of course not," Elle said. "And that's *not* my contest entry. I haven't figured out what I'm going to make yet."

"You haven't?" Chessie said. "There's not much time left. What are you waiting for? Inspiration? You know, Elle, inspiration never comes to some people. They're just not creative enough. I wouldn't wait around if I were you. Just try to muddle through as best you can."

"I've already got my entry all ready to go," Nica said. "It's incredibly hot. I'd like to give the rest of you a fighting chance, but I don't really see how I can avoid winning."

"If I can't win, I definitely want you to win, Nica," Chessie said. "And then you, Elle. But Nica has to win so she can help her father promote his wildlife visitors' center and save the seals."

"That center isn't going to save the seals," Elle said. "Building it drove them away!"

"What's the matter with you?" Chessie said. "Didn't you see it on the news? Nica's dad is doing a good thing!"

"Of course she saw it on the news," Nica said. "She was in the same news report . . . making a complete fool out of herself."

"That's right," Chessie said. "Elle, you know what they say: if it's on the news it has to be true."

"I used to think that way, too," Elle said. "But now I know it's not true. I know that for sure— from personal experience."

"Whatever," Nica said. "It doesn't matter, because you can't beat me in the bikini-design contest. You might as well drop out right now."

"Never," Elle said.

"Elle's no quitter, that's for sure," Chessie said. "She never gives up no matter how hopeless things are or how dumb she looks. She's like the Energizer

Bunny . . . just keeps going and going . . ."

"And going," Elle said. "I'm going right now." She picked up Underdog and retreated under her umbrella.

"Poor Elle," Chessie said. "She can't surf; she can't do much of anything right—and she tries so hard."

Elle covered her face with her hat. She was beginning to wonder if Chessie was right. Lately nothing she did seemed to work. But that didn't matter. She couldn't give up. She had no choice. She had to give her all for Sassy, even if it was in vain.

Chapter 15

"ELLE, DARLING, you've been moping around the house all evening," Eva said. She stood in Elle's doorway dressed in a low-cut silver-sequined gown, her hair and makeup perfectly done. Wyatt stood next to her looking equally nice. Elle lay on top of her ruffled pink bedspread stroking Underdog and listening to sad music. "I can't stand to leave you like this. Wyatt, maybe we shouldn't go out tonight."

"Not go to the Plastic Surgeons' Annual Awards dinner?" Wyatt said. "But I'm up for Scalpel of the Year!"

"But look at her."

Elle lifted her head in a lame attempt to show her parents that she was all right. She wasn't really that sad, she told herself. She was just incubating ideas, letting them brew in her mind. Soon a brilliant one would appear to her like magic. She felt sure of it. But in the meantime, she was lying low.

"Please don't cancel your plans on my account," Elle said. "Go, go. Dad's going to win Scalpel of the Year. You can't miss that."

Wyatt walked to the bed and brushed Elle's hair out of her face to get a good look at her. "I see what you mean, Eva. She's looking pretty pale for someone who spends all day at the beach."

"You two go, I'll take care of her." Zosia appeared in the hallway behind them. "We're in luck: I know the perfect cure for peakedness, the blahs, the blues, or what have you. And it's coming on TV tonight. In ten minutes, as a matter of fact."

"What is it?" Wyatt asked.

"The Miss Galaxy contest," Zosia said. "What could be better for a troubled mind than a beauty pageant? The most mindless of all TV genres. In Europe, the great thinkers and philosophers watch them in order to clear their thoughts."

Elle sat up. "That sounds like exactly what I need. I'll make the popcorn, Zosia. Meet you in your room in ten."

"You see? It's already working," Zosia said.

"Thank you, Zosia," Eva said. "Now you know why we keep you on even though you can't cook or clean."

"We'll be back around one," Wyatt said.

"Have fun!" Elle called on her way to the kitchen.

Elle brought a big bowl of popcorn into Zosia's room and sat with her on the bed. Underdog jumped up and curled himself around Elle's feet. The contestants, one hundred young women from one hundred different countries, paraded out onto the stage wearing sashes over their dresses indicating where they were from and lip-synching to an insipid musical number.

"Look at Miss Latvia," Zosia said about a leggy, busty, blue-eyed blonde. "Those Baltic girls are strong every year."

"Did you ever compete in the Miss Galaxy contest?" Elle asked.

"Me? No. I never made it that far. But I *was* Miss Ironworks. And Miss Fishmonger."

"And Miss Gdańsk," Elle said.

"That's right."

"Wow," Elle said.

"You know how they make their teeth so shiny?" Zosia said. "Vaseline. They smear it across their teeth so they gleam in the TV lights."

Zosia was right; the beauty pageant was brain cleansing, in a funny and kind of addictive way. The girls promenaded across the screen in evening gowns and answered questions about how they would solve all the world's problems. Then came the swimsuit competition. Elle perked up and paid more careful attention.

Some of the contestants wore one-piece suits, but many wore bikinis. Elle watched them walk. Their bikini bottoms stayed put no matter how much the wearers wiggled their hips. It was remarkable. It was as if their suits were sprayed on.

"How do they do that?" Elle asked. "How do they keep their suits in place like that?" The suits were all perfect. Not one was riding up. And some of those suits were pretty skimpy.

"Simple," Zosia said. "Double-sided tape. They all use it."

"Double-sided tape?"

"You know, it's sticky on both sides. One side sticks to the swimsuit, the other to the skin. If you do it right, it holds everything in place and no one sees how."

"That's it," Elle murmured, mostly to herself. "That's what I'll do. Forget a regular bikini—I'll make the perfect *surfing* bikini—one that doesn't move, no matter what you do. You can play volley-ball, surf, just walk down the beach—and your bikini stays put! It is exactly what SurfChix is look-ing for!"

"It's a good idea," Zosia said. "Everybody wants a suit that stays put."

"Especially me," Elle said. She gave Zosia a hug. "You were right—beauty pageants are the answer to everything. They can make you brilliant!"

Elle bought the strongest double-sided tape she could find and stuck it inside one of her bikinis. She tested it in the bathtub. And that's when the big problem appeared. The tape didn't work when it was wet.

"That *is* a problem," Laurette said later that day as they sat on the beach under Elle's umbrella. Elle had told her about the idea as Laurette strummed her guitar. "Especially since wetness is what surfing is pretty much all about."

"But the basic idea is good," Elle said. "A suit that doesn't slip or slide or untie or break. A true sports bikini that looks sexy, too. If only I could find a way to make it work."

"That's a pretty big if," Laurette said.

"Yoo-hoo." Chessie popped her head under the

umbrella. "I was walking by and couldn't help overhearing. Did you say something about double-sided tape?"

"What do you do, lurk outside our umbrella as soon as we put it up?" Laurette said.

"I don't lurk," Chessie said. "It's a free beach. I can stand on the other side of your umbrella if I feel like it. It's not my fault you guys talk loud enough for me to hear everything."

From under her umbrella, Elle saw two long, tanned feet, with a silver toe ring on the middle toe of one, walking in their direction. It had to be Nica. Chessie confirmed it.

"Nica, Elle's cheating," Chessie said. "She's going to use double-sided tape in the bikini contest."

"It's not cheating," Elle said. "Where in the rules does it say you can't use tape? Show me."

Nica ducked her head under the umbrella. "That's not a bad idea. Maybe I'll try it. Just to make my fabulous bikini that much better."

"Go ahead," Elle said. "It doesn't work."

"She's probably just saying that to stop you from doing it," Chessie said.

"No, I'm not," Elle said. "Try it yourself. The tape unsticks in the water."

"You know what?" Nica said. "I will try it.

Because if it works, I don't think it would be fair for you to have an advantage."

"It was her idea," Laurette said. "Her only advantage was superior brainpower."

"Brainpower's not much use if you have no sense of style," Nica said. "At least when it comes to design contests."

"Hey—I have a sense of style," Elle protested.

"Yeah—canine style," Nica said, casting a glance at Underdog. Elle was glad she hadn't dressed him up that day. "And come to think of it, *I'm* going to find a way to make my bikini stay in place, even if the tape doesn't work. The judges will love the practicality."

"You can't do that!" Elle said. "That's my idea."

"What? Do you have a patent on it?" Nica said.

"No," Elle admitted.

"Then it's up for grabs, isn't it," Nica said.

Elle frowned. Nica was so frustrating!

"Don't worry, Elle," Laurette said. "She'll try the tape, see that it doesn't work, and give up. While you think of another brilliant idea, with your *brainpower*, and win the contest!"

"That's a nice fairy tale," Nica said. "Maybe I'll tell it to my grandchildren when I get old."

"Oh, Nica," Chessie said, "don't be silly. You

know you're never going to get that old."

"Are you saying I'm going to die young?" Nica asked.

"No!" Chessie looked alarmed. "I meant that no matter what your age, you'll always be young . . . looking . . . and at heart."

"Oh," Nica said. "I guess that's okay. Sorry I snapped. I'm a little jumpy lately."

If this is a little jumpy, I'd hate to see her really jumpy, Elle thought, before turning her attention to the beach and brainstorming . . . again.

Chapter 16

"HERE SHE is." Paula Kramer, the Malibu wildlife ranger, let Elle, Laurette, and Underdog into the Marine Mammal Habitat, a sunny area with a saltwater pool, sand, and rocks to simulate a real beach. Sassy sat on a rock, sunning herself. Underdog gave a little bark. Sassy growled happily at the sight of company.

"She's gotten bigger," Elle said, and it was true. Sassy had grown in the last few weeks and looked a little less like a baby. But she was still smaller than she should have been, and obviously vulnerable.

"We feed her and play with her," Paula said. "But she's longing for her mother. You can tell by the way she has to be coaxed into eating. And she isn't as playful as a healthy seal pup should be."

"That is so sad," Laurette said.

"Can we pet her?" Elle asked.

"Sure," Paula said, "for a minute."

Elle held Underdog and perched beside Sassy on the rock. She and Laurette gently stroked Sassy's head.

"Poor Sassy," Elle said. "We check the seal cove every day for signs of the other seals, but they haven't been there. Do you think Sassy's mother will ever come back?"

"Not as long as there's construction going on nearby," Paula said. "Until you stop that building, the seals will stay away. They're afraid of all that noise and activity."

"If Mr. Saunders builds his development, Seal Beach will always be noisy," Laurette said.

"And the humans will scare the seals away, too," Paula added.

Sassy slipped off the rock and swam through the water, jumping and flapping about. The water rippled off her skin.

"If only my bathing suit could fit me as well as her skin fits her," Elle said. "That would be the perfect bikini to win the contest."

Laurette laughed. "Yeah. You'd win for sure.

But that would be impossible. I mean, you'd have to surf naked. Are you ready to do that?"

"No," Elle said. "Are you crazy? Anyway, surfing naked doesn't involve much design talent."

"I know," Laurette said. "You could *say* that you've designed the perfect, unbudgeable bikini, made from the finest cloth. And I'll go around saying to everyone, 'Hey, isn't that the coolest bikini you ever saw? Of course, only superchic people can see it. People with bad taste can't see a thing!' Only, you'll be naked."

"Laurette—"

"But everyone will be afraid to admit that they can't see your bikini," Laurette said, "because they'll think it means they have bad taste."

"But—"

"So everyone will say your suit is the best," Laurette said, "and out of total terror and fear of being exposed for having bad taste, they'll award you first place!"

"You mean like 'The Emperor's New Clothes'?" Elle said.

"Exactly," Laurette said.

"But it still requires me to walk around naked in front of everybody, on national TV."

"Come on, Elle, you can hack it."

"Sorry, Laurette. I can't do it. Why don't you try it? I'll tell everyone you're my model."

"That's okay," Laurette said. "My self-esteem hasn't progressed to those heights yet."

"It was a good idea, though," Elle said. "In theory."

"Hitting the pipeline today, Elle?" Sunrise asked. Elle sat at the counter of the Surf Shack and sipped a cup of hot tea. She and Underdog had arrived at the beach early that morning to get some more surfing practice in. She looked at the overcast sky and the dark, calm water and shivered.

"I don't know," Elle said. "It's so chilly today."

"That's true," Sunrise said. "Business is going to be slow today. Only the hard-core crew shows up when it's cloudy and chilly. I doubt we'll be seeing your friend Chessie this morning."

Elle scanned the horizon. "Hunter's already out there. And Clive and Aquinnah. And Nica."

Of course, Nica. She was determined to win the surfing contest . . . and all the other contests she'd entered, for that matter.

"I really need to work on my chops," Elle said. "I haven't managed to get up and ride a wave for more than a few seconds. But I hate being cold."

Underneath her long-sleeved T-shirt and cotton pants, Elle had on only a bikini. She couldn't imagine lasting long in the chilly water with practically nothing on.

"So, get out there," Sunrise said. "I know it's cold. That's why man invented wet suits."

"Wet suits?" Elle said.

"Sure," Sunrise said. "What do you think they're all wearing out there, Speedos?"

Elle looked more carefully at the surfers in the water. They *were* more covered up than usual. The boys wore slick black or orange wet suits. Aquinnah's was hot pink, and Nica's was kind of a psychedelic blue pattern. Very sixties. Elle thought it must have been made by the famous Italian designer Pucci.

"I've got one in your size," Sunrise said. She reached under the counter and pulled out a small blue rubber suit. The bottoms stopped at the knee and the top had long sleeves. "This will keep you warmer in cold water than that bikini. Why don't you try it on?"

"You'll lend it to me?" Elle asked.

"Sure," Sunrise said. "Rental is free with every purchase of a carrot-sunflower muffin."

"One carrot-sunflower muffin, please," Elle said.

Sunrise toasted one and gave it to Elle on a plate with butter.

Elle wolfed down the muffin and finished her tea. Sunrise showed her how to put the suit on properly, rolling it on over her bikini.

"How does that feel? Comfy?" Sunrise asked.

"Perfect," Elle said.

"Good. Now get out there and shred the place up! Underdog and I will watch you from here."

"Thanks, Sunrise." Elle picked up her board and ran to the shore. The waves were breaking nicely— not scary-huge, but big enough for a good ride. She watched the others darting this way and that over the foam in their wet suits and thought of Sassy. *They look like seals out there*, she thought, marveling at how comfortable they all looked in the water, especially Hunter. *Seals at play*, she thought. She made a little growling sound like Sassy and said, "Look out, another seal is coming out into the water to play!"

She ran into the surf and paddled out to the lineup. Hunter sat on his board, waiting for a good curl. "Hey, Elle!" he called when she joined the group. "Now the hard-core gang is all accounted for."

Nica, who was also sitting in the lineup, snorted. "Yeah, right. Hard-core. I think you have to have actually mastered the act of *surfing* to be considered hard-core, don't you?"

"Can it, Nica," Clive said. "You can be a nasty little snipe when you want to!"

"Nasty is as nasty does," Nica said, turning her board around in anticipation of a nice, juicy wave. "Watch this."

She caught the wave, which curled around her like a tunnel. She zigzagged expertly across it, sinking at last into the foam feet first.

"Nice one," Hunter said.

Clive whistled. "She's got me there."

"I'll never be able to surf like that," Elle said.

"Yes you will," Hunter said. "Today's the perfect day to practice. The water's not crowded, so you've got plenty of room and plenty of waves to yourself."

Elle noticed that she felt nice and toasty in her wet suit. In fact, it fit her so well, she forgot she had it on.

"Turn around, Elle," Hunter said. "Here comes a good one."

Elle spun around on her board and got into paddling position. She glanced back at the approaching wave. It was bigger than she would have liked. In fact, it was the biggest one she'd ever tried to ride.

Hunter floated next to her and gave her a

shove. "You can do it, Elle! Paddle! Paddle! Go!"

Elle paddled as hard as she could. She felt the wave swell up behind her and stood up on her board. "Lean forward!" Hunter yelled. She leaned forward, and the wave carried her along. Her stance was sturdy. She held out her arms for balance. She was doing it! She was riding one! She was surfing!

She shifted her weight as needed and kept her balance. It didn't feel as if the water were moving under her. It felt as if she and her board were part of the water. She was a little water mammal like Sassy, completely at home in her salty element.

Her mind cleared; she didn't think. She didn't worry about straps or tops falling off or bottoms riding up or sand or anything. Something clicked inside her, and she knew: she had gotten it. She had finally gotten it. She didn't think she could ever describe it or teach it to anyone else. But at last she was a surfer!

Before she knew it, the ride was over. She glided up to the shore until her board couldn't go any farther. Then she stepped off, in total control. She had done it! She could surf now!

From out on the lineup, Hunter, Clive, and Aquinnah were cheering and whistling. "Woo-hoo!

All right, Elle! Way to rip it, girl!"

Elle turned around and paddled right back out.

"Way to lay pipe!" Clive said.

"You did it!" Hunter said, giving her a kiss when she reached the lineup. "I told you you could."

"I'm stoked!" Elle shouted. "Let's do it again!"

She sat on her board, watching the horizon for another good curl. "How's that wet suit working for you?" Aquinnah asked.

Elle glanced down at the blue rubber suit. She'd forgotten she was wearing it. That's the secret, she realized. That's why it finally clicked. Because I forgot about my bikini and being modest and what I looked like and just let myself go. Because the wet suit fits me like a glove. Like skin! Like Sassy's skin fits her.

"It's working pretty good," Elle said. "Wicked good. Gnarly good. It's pumping!"

"We get the point," Nica said.

"Another swell, coming up," Hunter said. "Take it, Elle!"

Elle paddled, caught the wave, and rode it in, even better than she had the last one. All day long she surfed wave after wave. Now that she had gotten it, she never wanted to stop.

Chapter 17

"YOUR FIRST ride!" Laurette exclaimed. "I wish I could have been there to see it. But it was too chilly for the beach yesterday. What made you go?"

"I don't know," Elle said. She'd invited Laurette over to her house for a surprise. "But I'm so glad I did. The wet suit freed me. It didn't move. I forgot I was wearing it. It was like wearing nothing at all—almost like what we were saying before, the emperor's new clothes. Except I was the opposite of naked; I was almost completely covered up."

"Which makes the whole story much easier to take," Laurette said.

"Yes," Elle said. "And it gave me my brilliant idea. Look! Ta-da!"

Elle had raced home from surfing the day before, exhilarated. On her way home, she'd stopped at a fabric store and a surf-supply shop. Then she had locked herself in her room, as was her habit, and spent much of the night and the next day making this: her first prototype of the Seal Suit.

"What is it?" Laurette said, taking the chunky orange rubber thing out of Elle's hands and holding it up for a better look.

"It's a bikini made out of wet-suit material," Elle said. "I call it the Seal Suit. The rubber stays in place so well it's kind of hard to get off, to be honest. But staying on is what counts. It will stay put in a hurricane. You could spray water from a fire hose at it and it wouldn't budge."

"But it's so thick," Laurette said. "And why is it orange? That's not really your color."

"I looked at lots of wet suits," Elle said. "I figured I'd cut one up and make a bikini out of it. This was the thinnest suit I could find. It only came in orange." She was unhappy with the color herself. Only a very tanned person could look good in orange, and Elle hadn't achieved high tannage yet. Even spray-on might not be enough to help her achieve the complexion needed to pull off an orange suit. Her mother had had Elle's color chart done when Elle turned thirteen, and Elle had been warned not to wear orange, or she would risk looking like a corpse. Orange was a spring or fall color, and Elle was definitely more suited to summer fashions.

"Let me see it on you," Laurette said.

Elle disappeared into the bathroom and put on the bikini. She walked stiffly back into the bedroom.

"It looks weird," Laurette said. "Like the Michelin Man in his underwear. Kind of lumpy."

Elle sighed. Maybe the rubber *was* too thick.

"I don't know what else to do," she said. "This was the best wet-suit rubber I saw. There's got to be a way to make it work. If only I could find something prettier and thinner, with more stretch, but not too much . . . But what?"

"I don't know," Laurette said. "But I'm afraid this isn't working. Sure, the bikini stays on, but it has to look good, too, right?"

"How could making a bikini be so hard?" Elle wailed. "I have newfound respect for bathing-suit designers. They must be geniuses."

She sat on the bed and idly glanced at her nails. Several of them were chipped from handling all the sticky rubber.

"What I need is another visit to Pamperella,"

she said. Just uttering the words made her feel better. "My manicure is a disgrace." The prospect of a trip to the salon never failed to make things look brighter.

"You always seem to get great ideas at the salon," Laurette said. "I wished it worked that way for me. I feel as if the longer I sit there being buffed and polished, the dumber I get."

"Not me," Elle said. "It's something about Bibi. Whatever your problem is, she talks to you until you see the answer that was right under your nose all along."

"You'd better make an appointment right away," Laurette said, "because the bikini contest is in three days. Whatever answers you've got waiting under your nose, it's time to find them."

"Oh, sweetie, I wish I could help you." Bibi took the rollers out of Elle's hair and applied styling gel to hold the wave. "But I'm no good at these things. Designey things, I mean. I have no eye."

"That isn't true," Elle said. "You're a genius at picking out the right nail color, and the right haircut for someone's face. Your highlights are a work of art." Elle picked up a strand of her own blonde hair and waved it at Bibi as proof. "But it doesn't matter, anyway. I need to find my own perfect bikini design, all by myself. No one can help me, not really."

"Clear your mind," Bibi said, brushing out Elle's wavy new do. "Just relax and let the hairbrush do its work. Something will come."

Elle closed her eyes, but all she could see was Sassy's sad little face at the wildlife refuge, and that was too painful, so she opened them again. She looked idly around the salon. Another stylist was brushing a client's hair with dye; she wore hot-pink latex gloves to protect her hands. Hot pink was Pamperella's official color, and everything in the salon that could be pink was, from the stylists' smocks to the stationery the bills were printed on.

The stylist's nimble fingers mesmerized Elle. The gloves protected her hands but didn't restrict her at all, Elle noticed. Interesting.

Then Bibi stood in front of her, blasting her with the hair dryer and blocking Elle's view of the room. "Tilt your head down," Bibi ordered, and Elle did as she was told. She looked down at Bibi's silver skirt. It peeked out from under her smock, which Bibi had left unbuttoned. It was tight and shiny and looked slightly stretchy.

"Pretty skirt," Elle shouted over the blow-dryer.

"Thanks." Bibi turned the dryer off and examined

Elle's hair. "You can lift your head now."

"What is it made of?" Elle asked.

"Latex," Bibi said. She moved behind Elle to brush out her hair.

"Wait," Elle said. "Come back." She spun herself around in her chair so that she faced Bibi.

"What are you doing, honey? I need to give the back of your hair some lift."

"Can I touch it?" Elle asked.

"Your hair?"

"No. Your skirt."

Bibi looked at her as if the hair-spray fumes might have gone to her head. "Go ahead. Whatever turns you on."

Elle tugged at the hem of Bibi's skirt. It gave slightly, but didn't really move. She pinched it. It was almost rubbery, and very thin.

"Okay, don't think I'm weird or anything," Elle said. "But would you mind taking off your smock and walking across the room?"

Bibi squinted, but she took off her smock. "Elle, I think you've been out in the sun too long."

"Trust me, I have a good reason," Elle said.

Bibi stood in front of her in a white tank top and the silver latex skirt, which hugged her like a second skin. She sauntered from her station to the shampoo sinks in her silver spike heels. Her hips swayed appealingly from side to side. The skirt clung to her for dear life. She turned around and walked back.

Bibi tugged at the hem of the skirt. "If I don't wear panty hose under it, it sticks to my legs," she said. "But I hate panty hose."

"Oh, my God," Elle said. "I think I've got it."

"It's not contagious, is it?" Bibi asked.

"No, I mean, I think I've got the answer," Elle said. "The perfect material to make a sexy, stay-in-place bikini. It comes in lots of cool colors like hot pink and silver. It sticks to your skin but it moves with your body. It's so thin it's like a second skin. Latex!"

Bibi flicked the blow-dryer off and on in delight. "That's brilliant! And you know what? I think it will work."

"I think it will, too," Elle said.

"Just make sure you line it where it counts, if you know what I mean," Bibi said. "This stuff really does stick to your skin."

"I will," Elle said. "Where did you buy that skirt?"

"At this boutique on Sunset called Latex Kitten," Bibi said. "You might think it's a little weird in there. But it's the best place to buy latex clothes.

They even sell latex ball gowns."

"Thanks, Bibi!" Elle jumped out of the chair and kissed Bibi on the cheek. "You've done it again. You're a miracle worker!"

Elle was so excited she ran out of the salon. She couldn't wait to get to Latex Kitten.

"That's very nice of you, but wait!" Bibi called, running after her. "I haven't finished puffing up your hair!"

"It'll just de-puff in the car." Elle cried. "See you next week!"

Chapter 18

"OKAY, HERE goes." Elle stepped out onto the patio covered by a robe. "The first test drive of the new Elle Woods Seal Suit."

The audience—Laurette, Zosia, and Bernard—clapped in anticipation. Elle took off the robe to reveal her new bikini, made out of lovely pink latex. It was trimmed in white, and the halter top was anchored by a big pink peony at the nape of her neck.

"Stunning!" Zosia cheered.

"Perfect," Laurette said.

"Very fine," Bernard said. "But what happens when you dive into the pool?"

"That's what we're about to find out." Elle

stepped up on the diving board. She did a test jump, then prepared to dive. She took three steps and a preparatory hop, then dived into the pool. She swam a few strokes. The latex stuck to her skin as she glided smoothly through the water.

When she came up for air, everyone clapped again. Elle pulled herself out of the water and checked the bikini. Everything was in place. Nothing had moved. And she'd hit the water with enough impact to pull her usual bikini top right off.

"It worked!" she cried.

"You still have to try surfing in it," Laurette warned.

"True," Elle said, "but the Seal Suit passed the first test. And I have confidence. Now for the fashion element. Any suggestions?"

"I love the flower," Laurette said.

"I like the white trim," Bernard said. "It emphasizes the suit's form and line."

"I like the cut," Zosia said. "Sexy, but not too bare. But tell me, Elle—when are you going to get your spray tan?"

"Tomorrow," Elle said, "the morning of the contest. So it will be nice and fresh."

"Good," Zosia said. "Then everything is set. Elle, if you don't win, that contest is fixed."

"You know, that *is* a possibility," Laurette said. "Considering you're competing against the daughter of the greediest developer in SoCal."

"Fixed?" Elle said. "No way. It can't be fixed. How could you fix a contest like this?"

"Easy," Bernard said. "Bribe the judges."

"Nica wouldn't stoop that low," Elle said. "Would she? I mean, this isn't a spy movie. It's just the SurfChix contest."

"Anything is possible," Zosia said.

"Darling, what a cute bikini!" Eva Woods dropped several shopping bags at the door and breezed out to the patio, dressed in crisp white linen pants, a pastel top, plenty of gold jewelry, and strappy sandals. She'd just come back from shopping.

"Thanks, Mom," Elle said. "I made it myself."

Eva shook her head in admiration. "My little prodigy."

Elle began to dig through Eva's shopping bags. "What did you get today, Mom? Anything good?"

"Elle, aren't you friends with that Saunders girl—what's her name? Nica?" Eva asked.

"I don't know if I'd say we're friends—" Elle said.

"She's one of your surf buddies, isn't she?" Eva said.

Elle glanced at Laurette. "Well, she surfs, and I know her. Why?"

"The funniest thing," Eva said. "I was at the Zola Plunkett trunk show at Barneys this afternoon— you know, she makes *adorable* swimsuits, some of the nicest I've ever seen. I actually bought four of them today. They're somewhere in those bags if you want to see them. The colors and patterns are ultrachic, and the fit is incredible, even for an old lady like me."

Eva turned to Zosia for the customary denial that she was an old lady—it was part of Zosia's job, just as backing up all of Wyatt's glamorized memories of his youth was part of Bernard's.

"But, Mrs. Woods, no one would ever call a beautiful, fit, youthful woman like you an old lady," Zosia said dutifully—though it was perfectly true. Elle's mother took good care of herself and was very attractive. And the fact that her husband was one of Beverly Hills's leading plastic surgeons didn't hurt. "You're beautiful."

"Thank you, Zosia. How kind of you to say that," Eva said.

"Mom, what does all this have to do with Nica?" Elle said.

"Well, I overheard one of Zola's assistants when

she was talking about a top secret Saunders project.Apparently she's designing a bikini exclusively for your friend Nica. Isn't that exciting?"

"Exciting?" Elle was stunned. She knew exactly what that meant. "Nica's father must be paying Zola Plunkett to design a suit for her."

"Well, of course, darling," Eva said. "I imagine he's paying her quite a bit. How else would you get a famous designer like Zola to make something exclusively for you? Unless you're superclose friends, or related. Maybe they are related! That would be even more exciting!"

"Mom, it's not exciting, it's terrible!" Elle cried.

"Don't be envious, Elle," Eva said. "That's not like you. I think it's lovely that your friend Nica knows the fabulous Zola. And I have a terrific idea. Why don't we have them all over here one evening: Nica, her parents, and Zola. We'll have cocktails!"

"Cocktails!" Elle cried. "Mom, we can't celebrate with them! Nica is cheating!"

"Dear, we all do what we must to be fabulous," Eva said. "I don't consider it cheating."

"But she is doing it in the SurfChix bikini design contest," Elle said. "I designed this bikini so I can win the contest and save the seals at Seal Beach.

But Nica wants to win, too. And she's using a ringer—a professionally designed bikini. It's not fair."

Eva ran her eyes over Elle's bikini. "Dear, I hate to break it to you, but although your bikini is perfectly sweet, I'm not sure it can compete with a Zola."

"That's my point!" Elle cried. "Nica has an unfair advantage."

"But what can you do about it?" Zosia asked. "The contest is tomorrow."

"And even if you told the judges, how could you prove it?" Laurette said. "Just saying that your mother overheard something in a department store isn't going to cut it."

Elle frowned and sat down on a chaise longue. "I don't believe this. Mr. Saunders will do anything to get what he wants." She sighed and rested her head in her hands. "I guess I'll just have to hope that the activity part of the contest saves me."

"The activity part?" Laurette said. "You mean, the surfing part?"

"That's what I've chosen to do," Elle said. The SurfChix company was known for activewear, and they insisted that each entrant in the bikini contest show off her suit while performing some kind of beach activity. The point was to demonstrate that the bikini not only looked good, but was comfortable, durable, well made, and practical as well. "I figured if they saw how well my suit works in the water, it would help me win."

"But Nica is going to surf, too," Laurette said. "You just learned to surf the other day. And she's practically a pro. Elle, you're doomed."

Elle shook her head. Nothing could keep her down for long. "You never know. Maybe Nica will wipe out. Maybe her suit will dissolve in water like an Alka-Seltzer. It ain't over until it's over."

She saw Laurette glance at Zosia and Bernard and knew what they were thinking: *Oh, it's over, baby.*

"Look," Elle said. "It's not hopeless. Maybe Hunter will win the surfing competition. And maybe Warp Factor Five will win the Battle of the Bands. You can speak out for Sassy on my behalf. It's better than nothing."

"Of course I will—if we win," Laurette said. "Which is hardly a given. We've got our last rehearsal tonight, and if Mike the drummer doesn't stop rushing the beat, we're history."

"Well," Elle said, deflating slightly, "there's always Hunter."

"He'll win for sure," Eva said. "He's so adorable. How could he not win?"

"It's not a male beauty contest," Laurette said. "He has to outsurf Nica. And Brett and Clive. And some of the best surfers from all over the country. It won't be easy."

"He can do it," Elle said. "And so can you. And so can I. Just think how great it would be if we all won! A triple threat! Seal Beach would be saved for sure."

"It would be fantastic," Laurette said. "But I wouldn't get your hopes up."

Elle couldn't help it; she couldn't keep her hopes down. She knew that the forces of good and right were on her side.

Bernard rose and said, "I'd better get started on dinner. Mrs. Woods, I left some mail for you on your desk. There was something for you, too, Elle. It's on the kitchen table."

"Thanks, Bernard." Curious, Elle and Laurette followed him into the kitchen. Elle didn't get a whole lot of mail, since she saw most of her friends on a daily basis.

She found her mail on the kitchen counter. It was a large manila envelope addressed to *Miss Elle Woods*. There was no return address. Elle opened it.

"Laurette, look!"

Inside was an architect's rough sketch, signed by the architect himself, on his firm's official paper. It was a detailed layout of a large development project. It showed exactly where the houses and a marina would be built, how the sand would be dug up and moved to create a deeper cove, and how the hills beyond the beach would be carved up and flattened to make room for more houses. At the top were the words *Saunders Development Company Project #59343: Seal Beach*.

"Where did it come from?" Laurette asked.

Elle checked the envelope again. There was no return address, but there was a postmark: Sedona, Arizona. A spa town.

"I can't be sure," Elle said. "But I have a strong hunch. We've got an undercover friend in the Saunders camp."

"Marla?" Laurette asked.

Elle nodded.

Paper-clipped to the plans was a note.

> *Contact state senator Mel Heffernan's assistant, Chris Biden. She knows Sassy's story and wants to help. She can give you all the documentation you need. Some of Senator Heffernan's money has recently*

*been through the wash, if you know what
I mean.*

—Madame X

"Sassy's story did get through to someone," Elle said as the meaning of the note sank in. Someone cared. Someone was willing to help. All Elle needed to do was get this information out there.

"Elle—do you know what this is?" Laurette said. "It's exactly what you've needed all along. It's proof. We've got enough here to tear down half the state senate, I bet."

"Mr. Saunders will never get away with anything like this again," Elle said. "We're going to save Seal Beach!"

Laurette slapped her five.

Elle carefully put the note and the sketch back into the envelope. She had to keep them safe. She was going to bring them with her to the contest, where they might, she thought, come in very handy.

"I knew the forces of good would come through," she said. "They always do."

Chapter 19

"WELCOME TO the first annual SurfChix contest, sponsored by SurfChix." The MC's voice blared over the loudspeakers. "If you're on the move, SurfChix has got you covered."

This was it: the big day. Elle bounced nervously on her toes. She wished this day were just about winning or losing a design contest. She wished there weren't so much at stake.

Elle had never seen so many people at Seal Beach. The street was lined with cars and vans and TV trucks. Crowds surged along the beach, lined up at the Sunrise Surf Shack for food, and sat in beach chairs on the sand, waiting for the contests to begin.

A stage had been set up near the road, with a

full sound system and a big blue-and-white banner that read, SURFCHIX: SEAL BEACH. An announcer stood at the microphone, ready to start the proceedings. He had long hair and wore board shorts, a Hawaiian shirt, and a baseball cap. TV cameras pointed at him, then swiveled around to photograph the crowds sunbathing.

An aboveground swimming pool was set up near the stage, and people were batting a volleyball back and forth over one of three nets. It was a perfect day for a beach party: sunny and warm, with an onshore wind whipping up nice-sized waves.

"Thank you all for coming," the announcer said. "I'm Steve Glazer, and here is our lineup. We'll start with the surfing competition, since that takes the longest and the waves are rolling nicely this morning, followed by the SurfChix bikini design contest, in which each competitor will model her—or his—active bikini."

The crowd clapped, cheered, and woo-hooed for the bikini contest.

"And finally, throughout the day," Steve said, "right here on this stage, we have the Battle of the Bands to provide us with a sound track of rockin' surf tunes. We'll announce the winning band at the end of the day, and they'll play for us this evening at the SurfChix Beach Blanket Blowout, our celebration bonfire, feast, and dance-party extravaganza. It's going to be a great day at the beach, so stick around, and let 'er rip!"

Everyone cheered, and the games began.

Hunter clustered with the surfing competitors, his arm around Elle. She was wearing her Seal Suit, hidden under a cute white terry-cloth cover-up decorated with yellow daisies. Her newly tanned body glistened in the sun, thanks to a good dose of spray-on tan and bronzer.

A SurfChix representative explained how the surf contest would work. There were thirty contestants divided up for ten heats of three surfers each. Each heat would last twenty minutes. The surfers in each heat would be identified by the color of their rash guards: red, white, or yellow. They'd be graded on how many waves they caught and the quality of their rides. Hunter, wearing a red rash guard, was in the eighth heat, with Brett and Nica.

"Are you nervous?" Elle asked Hunter.

"A little," he admitted. "Are you?"

"A lot," she said.

"Don't be scared," Hunter said. "I'll be rooting for you."

"And I'll be rooting for you," Elle said.

Clive and Aquinnah surfed the first heat against a guy from San Diego. Elle cheered for both of them; she couldn't help herself. Of course, she wanted Hunter to beat them, but she wanted them to do well, too.

Aquinnah paddled frantically to catch a big curl headed her way. Clive and the San Diego guy just missed it. "She's caught a big one," Hunter said. "Go, girl!"

"Go, Aquinnah! Go!" Elle shouted. Aquinnah expertly steered her way along the curl, gracefully dismounting in the shallows. It was thrilling to see another girl surfing so beautifully.

"And Aquinnah Castro, in the yellow, should score major points for that beauty," Steve Glazer said.

"*Wooo!* All right!" Elle clapped and jumped up and down.

"You're going to be all cheered out by the time my heat comes up," Hunter said.

"I've always got cheers in reserve for you," Elle said.

Someone tapped Elle on the shoulder. Elle turned to see who it was, startled for a second at the sight of a glittery, heavily made-up girl she didn't recognize. Or did she?

"Elle, it's me," Laurette said.

"Wow! You look so glam," Elle said.

"I know," Laurette said. "It's for the contest. Darren thought we should go all out and really glam it up." She usually didn't wear much makeup. Or red-and-blue streaks sprayed into her hair. Or a tight, red-sequined bikini bra, with strips of red silk shredded to look like a hula skirt for the bottoms. She'd taken off her gold, spike-heeled sandals and was carrying them in one hand so she could walk on the beach without sinking into the sand.

"You look fantastic," Elle said. "Are you ready?"

"I hope so," Laurette said. "I practiced all night. I just hope we all stick together and don't lose the beat. Then we should be all right." She stared out at the water, where Clive was kicking serious surfer butt. "I've got a few hours to kill before we play. What's happening out here?"

"Clive and Aquinnah are neck and neck," Elle said. "The San Diego guy hasn't caught a wave yet."

"He'd better hurry," Hunter said. "He's two rides behind Clive and Aquinnah."

The San Diego guy never did catch a wave— it turned out he had a serious case of nerves. Aquinnah won the heat with a good score of 8.8. Clive was close behind with 8.6.

"Way to rip it!" Hunter said, giving Aquinnah and Clive high fives when they came back on shore.

"They're roaring out there," Clive said. "Better stretch out good before you go in."

Hunter started windmilling his arms and stretching out his legs while the contestants in the second heat took their turns. He lay down and Elle walked barefoot on his back to loosen up his muscles.

"Dude, you ready to get your butt kicked?" Brett Morton, in yellow, planted his feet on either side of Hunter's head. Hunter sputtered and spit out some sand.

"Step back," Elle said. "You're getting sand in his mouth."

"Oops. Sorry," Brett said. "But if I were you I'd just stay down there in the sand, Hunter. No point in getting up. You have no chance of beating me. I'm totally *on it* today. I can feel it. Muscles twitching like a tiger's. I got it *down*."

"You've also got mustard on your lip," Elle said. "Too bad they don't judge on neatness."

"You're in the bikini design contest, aren't you?" Brett said. "Got your bikini on under there? Let's see it."

He grabbed for the hem of Elle's coverall and tried to pull it up. She jerked away.

"No! Get away from me! It's top secret!" Elle cried.

Hunter leaped to his feet and pushed Brett away. "Don't touch her," he warned.

"Or what?" Brett sneered.

"Or you'll be sorry." Hunter towered over Brett. Elle could see in Brett's eyes that he was intimidated. But he was too macho to back down.

"So, your bikini is top secret?" Brett said. "Just like Nica's? Well, I've already seen Chessie's entry, and I think she's going to shock everybody and take you all. Or if not her, Nica. I don't know what *your* secret is, Elle, but whatever Nica's is, it's got to be good, knowing her dad and all."

"Thanks for the tip," Elle said. "Now let me give *you* one: you'd better wax your board soon, because your heat is about to start."

Brett stared at her for a second. He seemed confused by the fact that the tip she had given him was actually helpful and not sarcastic or mean.

"Okay," he said. "I'll do that." He walked over to his board. Chessie and Nica stood nearby. They waved to Elle. She waved back.

"There she is—the cheater," Laurette said.

"Are you talking about Nica or Chessie?" Hunter asked.

"Nica," Laurette said. "But I wouldn't rule Chessie out."

"Maybe Nica had a change of heart overnight," Elle said. "Maybe she decided that she didn't want to win by cheating. Maybe she realized it's better to win with her own hard work and good ideas, and maybe under that incredibly beautiful Pucci beach dress is an ordinary bikini, designed by a sixteen-year-old girl and not by a famous fashion icon, an ordinary bikini that, while nicely made, cannot possibly beat mine." She looked at Hunter and Laurette in search of assurance. None came.

"Yeah, and maybe three ghosts visited her last night and showed her the true meaning of Christmas," Laurette said. "But I wouldn't bet on it."

"It could happen," Elle said. "People have changes of heart all the time."

"In the movies, maybe," Laurette said. "Not in real life."

Chessie hurried over.

"I just wanted to wish you luck," Chessie said. "You, too, Hunter." She scanned Elle from head to toe. "Elle, is that a spray-on tan? Well, aren't you clever! You know, it almost looks real. If I wasn't so used to being at the beach and seeing *natural* tans all summer long, I'd hardly notice yours came from a can. Really! You're so smart. When the rest of us are all old and wrinkled, you'll still be your same pale, baby-faced self. Well, good luck!" She hurried back to the Nica-and-Brett camp.

"Boy," Laurette said. "Does she ever stop?"

"I don't think so," said Hunter. "And I'm pretty sure that when we are all wrinkled, she will still be going . . . the Energizer Bunny of ridiculous comments."

Chapter 20

"THE EIGHTH heat is about to begin," Steve Glazer said. "Surfers, take your marks."

Nica pulled the Pucci dress over her head to reveal a white rash guard and matching bikini bottoms. She was obviously saving her contest entry for later. Why risk messing it up in the surf competition?

Elle kissed Hunter. "Good luck! Grab some pipe and rip it to shreds!"

Hunter grinned. "I'll do my best."

He and Nica and Brett lined up, forming a sequence of red, white, and yellow. An air horn bleated, and they ran into the surf, boards at their sides.

Elle crossed her fingers. "Win it for Sassy," she

said under her breath. "You can do it, Hunter!"

The three contestants sat together in the lineup. It wasn't long before a great wave came along. They all paddled hard, but Nica got there first. She maneuvered in the pocket of the wave near the curl and zigzagged back and forth. Her form was great.

"White is looking good, folks," Steve Glazer said. Nica popped into the air and did a half turn. "An aerial! This girl's going to be the one to beat."

Nica slid to shore and stepped off her board to wild cheers and applause. "The score for that ride is nine point seven," Steve said. The crowd went crazy. It was the highest score so far that day. Nica paddled back out to the lineup.

"Here comes another big one," Laurette said as a giant curl loomed over Hunter's head.

"Go, Hunter, go!" Elle shouted. Brett and Hunter raced to catch the wave. Hunter got the inside position ahead of Brett, which gave him the right of way. But Brett wouldn't let the wave go. He popped up on his board and rode right into Hunter's path. The only way Hunter could avoid crashing into him was to bail out. He fell into the water as Brett rode the wave in.

"Did you see that?" Elle said. "Hunter had that wave."

"Interference!" Chessie shouted. "Hunter nearly crashed into my brother on that wave!"

The air horn sounded. "Interference!" Steve said. "The judges call Yellow the aggressor. Yellow will be penalized for that ride and given a warning. One more move like that, Yellow, and you will be disqualified."

"Boo! Unfair!" Chessie yelled.

By the time Brett paddled back out, Hunter had scored another wave. It was a beautiful pipe, curling high over his head. He did a cutback, an aerial, a floater, a reentry. The wave just kept going, and Hunter gathered speed as it drove him into the soup.

"This is a thing of beauty," Steve said. "I've counted six radical maneuvers so far. Seven. This guy's got more tricks up his sleeve than Merlin."

Hunter sped into shore with a *whoosh*. The crowd yelped and howled in appreciation. Hunter turned around and paddled back out without waiting to hear his score.

"Nine point eight!" Steve said. "That's the score to beat today."

Elle gripped Laurette's hand. "He's going to do it," she said. "I'm afraid to say it out loud in case it jinxes him, but I can't help myself."

"Look at this," Laurette said, her chin jutting out toward Nica, who was twirling like Tinker Bell on another stellar pipe.

"White is looking good again," Steve said. "Nice maneuvers . . . but she hasn't quite hit the critical section of the wave. Wave selection is important, too, and this one is a little shorter and smaller than the others. . . . Let's see what the judges say. . . ."

Nica rolled neatly in. It had been a nice ride, but not as spectacular as her first one.

"Oooh, nine point five," Steve said. "Try again, White. You've got ten more minutes to score the perfect ride. And here comes Yellow—Oh! Tough break."

Brett had caught a huge wave, but he got too far in front of it, and it came crashing down on him, knocking him off his board. He surfaced, grabbed his board, and quickly paddled back to the lineup. There wasn't much time left, and he still hadn't scored.

"Here comes a beauty," Steve said. "White and Red both pop up at the same time. They're taking the wave in opposite directions, so no interference is called. Wow, look at that!"

Hunter and Nica were riding the same wave, one speeding left and the other zipping right. They knew this might be their last chance. Everything was on the line.

Nica pulled out every trick she had. She popped into the air again and again, spinning and flipping. Hunter kept pace, breaking in and out of the wave like a Jet Ski, building power and speed as he went. They sailed into the shallows simultaneously, to ecstatic applause. Nica stepped off her board and bowed.

Behind them, Brett caught his last wave. But he'd been so busy watching the other two that he bobbled and wobbled gracelessly to a stop.

"White's last ride scores a nine point eight," Steve said. "The score for Yellow, six point two. And the score for Red: nine point nine!"

Everyone on the beach jumped with excitement. Elle ran toward Hunter. But before she got there, Brett stepped toward Hunter and actually kicked him in the butt!

"Whoa! Unsportsmanlike conduct!" Steve cried. "Folks, I have never seen a surfer behave like that in competition before. Let's see what the judges think of that. . . . Disqualified! Yellow is officially disqualified from the contest!"

Jeers, boos, and cheers sounded. Brett turned red and stalked away, disappearing into the crowd.

The air horn sounded. "End of the eighth heat!" Steve said. "Only two more to go. But these scores are going to be very tough to beat."

Elle jumped into Hunter's arms. "You were great!" she cried. "You're going to win!"

"You've got this contest locked up," Laurette said.

Hunter grinned. "We'll have to wait and see. There are still some wicked good surfers left to go."

Elle turned to Nica. "You were excellent, too. Fantastic! I never saw you surf better."

Instead of thanking Elle, Nica said, "Don't think you've beaten me, Elle. Hunter may have outscored me in surfing. But the bikini contest is coming up, and no one will beat me there."

She walked away, kicking sand in her wake.

"Um, sportsmanship? Hello?" Laurette said. "What's with these people? What happened to the mellow, free-spirited surf vibe you see in the movies?"

"I don't know," Elle said. "But I miss it. I guess it all goes out the window when there are big things at stake. Like land and money. And a colony of seals."

Chapter 21

WHEN THE surf competition was over, everyone broke for lunch while the judges tallied the score. Elle was so nervous she could hardly eat.

"What are you worried about?" Laurette said. "You already know Hunter's going to win. He got the highest scores of the day."

"But what if something goes wrong?" Elle said. "What if they disqualify him on some sort of technicality no one has ever heard of?"

"I don't think you need to worry about that," Laurette said. "Here—the tofu dogs are excellent today. Take a bite. You need your strength."

Elle took a bite, and it calmed her a little. Half an hour later, she'd finished two dogs herself.

Lunch was over, and the judges called everyone to the stage to announce the surfing winners.

"The judges' scores have been tallied," Steve said. "The results are in. So here we go. Third place goes to Dave Malkmus!"

The audience clapped. "We'll give out the trophies in a ceremony later, so I'll make this quick," Steve said. "In second place, Nica Saunders!"

Elle scanned the crowd for Nica, but didn't see her.

"And the winner of the first annual SurfChix surfing competition is: Hunter Perry!"

"Big shock," Brett said.

"You did it! I knew you could!" Elle hopped up and down, planting a kiss on Hunter's cheek with each hop. He was a lot taller than she was, so it took some pretty good jumping to reach him.

"The winner will receive his trophy in a ceremony at the end of the day," Steve said. "Better start working on your speech, Hunter." The audience laughed. "And now, stay tuned for the sexiest contest of the day, the bikini design competition, coming up in just fifteen minutes!"

Hunter grabbed Elle, picked her up, and swung her around. "You know who helped me win?" he said, still holding her. Elle shook her head. "You.

Teaching you to surf helped me understand my own strengths and weaknesses and work on them. It made me a better surfer."

"You're just saying that," Elle said. They rubbed noses.

"No, I'm not," he said. "I mean every word."

"That is supersweet," Elle said. "But the important thing is you won! Don't forget to mention Sassy and the seals when you get your trophy at the awards ceremony."

"I won't forget," Hunter said.

"Now all I have to do is beat Nica in the bikini contest," Elle said. "Or should I say, all I have to do is beat world-famous designer Zola Plunkett—and outsurf Nica, who came in second in the surfing contest."

"You can do it," Hunter said. "I've seen you work magic. I know you can do anything."

"Thanks." Elle gave him one more kiss before he lowered her back to the ground. "Guess I'd better go get ready."

"Good luck!"

Elle grabbed her surfboard and walked over to the stage, where the bikini design contestants were lining up. Steve Glazer paced the stage, microphone in hand, glancing at some note cards.

"Here we go! Time for the SurfChix bikini design contest, ladies and gentlemen. The contestants will walk across the stage, beauty-pageant style, and model their designs. Then each one will perform some kind of activity in her bikini to demonstrate its wearability. Judges will score each bikini on design, attractiveness, fit, and how well it holds up during volleyball, surfing, swimming, or what have you."

Elle lined up with the other girls to the left of the stage. A young woman gave each contestant a cloth number to hang around her neck. Elle got the lucky number seven, a good sign.

Nica and Chessie were lined up ahead of her, with numbers four and five. "Good luck," Elle said to them.

Nica said nothing. She didn't even bother to turn around. Chessie said, "Good luck to you, too, Elle. You deserve it. You're a good sport, so I know you won't make a big scene when you lose."

"Thanks," Elle said. "That's big of you."

"I try," Chessie said.

"All right, ladies," Steve said. "Remove your cover-ups!"

Elle pulled her terry-cloth tunic over her head. All the contestants revealed their bikinis. She couldn't help checking out the competition. There were a lot of cute bikinis all up and down the line.

Chessie's simple white string number was a little strange; it appeared she'd forgotten to sew up the edges. But maybe she was going for a rough, unfinished look, Elle decided. Of course, that idea was at odds with the fact that she'd monogrammed the suit, in a way; the top was made of two white triangles with a large initial embroidered in red on each—*F*, for Francesca, on the right, and *M*, for Morton, on the left. The bottoms were decorated with a large *FM* on the back.

And then there was Nica's. When Elle finally allowed herself to look at it she stifled a gasp. It was fantastic—way beyond what you'd expect a normal teenage girl to make—even an extremely talented teenage girl. Made of some kind of space-age fabric Elle had never seen before, it was stretchy, metallic, and shiny. The matching top and bottom had a sophisticated and beautiful pattern of uneven waves in magical colors: ocean blue, green, white, and silver.

The bottom was cut in the classic bikini shape. But the top was like half a halter, crisscrossing in front: one strap rose over the left shoulder and connected with the bandeau top on the right—a daring, asymmetrical look. The bandeau, which in Elle's experience often had a squishing effect, was somehow molded to make Nica's chest look bigger and rounder than it really was. It was a feat of engineering and lovely to look at, too.

Elle was glad she hadn't seen it before, because not even all the good thoughts or lucky number sevens in the world could have made her feel better at that moment. Elle Woods felt utterly hopeless. Seal Beach was doomed.

Chapter 22

"ALL RIGHT, let's have our contestants line up on stage!" Steve said.

Music played, and one by one the girls dutifully marched across the stage, stopped to pose, and lined up along the back. The audience clapped for each contestant as she appeared, but Nica got an especially enthusiastic ovation. Chessie got a laugh when she tripped over a loose nail.

Elle walked out in her bikini and high-heeled sandals, posed, and joined the lineup. A line of judges sat in the front row of the audience, marking their scorecards. So far, so good. Elle's latex bikini was comfortable and stayed in place well, and she felt confident wearing it. But she knew she faced some stiff competition from the other girls.

"Go, Elle!" Laurette, Darren, and Hunter called from the audience. Underdog barked happily. Laurette, who was holding him, helped him wave his little paw at Elle.

"Looking good, girls, looking good!" Steve said. Several flashbulbs popped. "I see some strong contenders. But as you know, looks alone are not enough. Your bikinis must look good as well as hold up under the tough, active life of a SurfChix girl. So let's talk to our first contestant. Number One, come over here to the mike."

A black-haired girl in an electric-blue bikini with star cutouts at the hips approached the mike. "What's your name?" Steve asked.

"Jessica," the girl said.

"And what activity are you going to do today?"

"I'm going to play beach volleyball."

"Beach volleyball! All right," Steve said. "Go to it."

Jessica bounded off the stage to the nearest volleyball net, where a friend of hers in an identical bikini waited. The girl spiked the ball and they knocked it back and forth with their hands. Elle watched carefully. Jessica's suit rode up in the back, as most suits would, and she was constantly tugging the top down. Not good. She dived for a tricky shot and came up covered in sand.

"Okay, time's up," Steve said. "Thank you, Jessica!" The audience applauded, and the judges scribbled notes. Elle wasn't worried about Jessica.

The next girl did water ballet in the above-ground pool that had been set up near the stage. Her suit sagged a little when it got wet. Another girl performed a fancy dive and actually lost her top. She quickly grabbed it and pulled it back on underwater before she surfaced. She received some enthusiastic applause and whistles.

"That's a shame, Hannah, but nice save," Steve said. "Next, contestant number four."

Number four was Nica. She sauntered over to the mike, full of confidence. "My name is Nica Saunders, and my father, Fred Saunders, wants to build a wonderful observation area to help the seals, right here at Seal Beach!"

"That's nice, Nica," Steve said. "But there will be plenty of time for speeches after the contest. What's your activity?"

"I'm going to surf," Nica said.

"Good. And from what I've seen, you lay some excellent pipe," Steve said. "Go to it!"

Nica jumped off the stage, grabbed her board, and ran into the sea. The audience turned and followed her to the shallows to watch. The contestants watched from the stage.

Nica paddled out and sat for just a minute before a nice curl came and picked her up. She rode it in, twisting and turning to show off the way her bikini looked good from every angle. Her board stalled in chest-high water, and she jumped off and dragged her board to shore.

As she climbed out of the surf, her suit looked great, except for that one asymmetrical strap. It had slipped slightly down her shoulder as she was surfing. Elle caught her tugging it up before she bowed to the judges and waved to the audience, confident of victory.

"Wasn't she great?" Chessie said. "She's just so . . . so *perfect*. I'm so glad I'm friends with her."

Nica's suit glittered and flashed in the sun more than ever, now that it was wet. Elle had to admit Nica had made an excellent presentation. The suit was amazing, and Nica's surfing was flawless.

"Nica Saunders, everybody!" Steve said as Nica took another bow. "Very impressive. Up next, number five!"

"That's me!" Chessie cried.

Elle held her breath as Chessie walked up to the mike. Would she trip and fall on her face? No, she actually made it all the way to the front of the stage without incident. Way to go, Chessie, Elle thought.

"Your name is . . . let me guess; it starts with an *F*," Steve said, reading the initials off Chessie's top.

"That's right," Chessie said. "My name is Francesca Morton."

"And what is your activity, Francesca?"

"I'm going to do what bikinis were invented for," Chessie said. "Sunbathe!"

She stumbled off the stage—she wouldn't have been Chessie if she'd made it that far without doing something klutzy—and grabbed a fluffy yellow towel she'd stashed in a special spot. She spread the towel out and sat down on it, her feet perched daintily at the edge. Then she lay on her back and closed her eyes.

"Is that it?" Steve asked.

"No," Chessie said. "Look! I can turn onto my tummy!"

She rolled over onto her stomach, showing off the big red *FM* embroidered on the back of her suit. She kicked her feet playfully in the air.

"And *that's* it?" Steve asked.

"That's it," Chessie said. "What more could you want? My suit is specially designed to give a great tan with the fewest possible lines."

"Good job," Steve said. Chessie stood and folded up her towel to halfhearted applause. "Sunbathing is certainly an activity, of a sort. Okay, next!"

Elle felt sorry for Chessie. Her presentation had been about as lame as could be, and yet Chessie seemed totally unaware of its lameness.

Maybe she's so sure Nica will win she didn't bother trying, Elle thought, though the proud smile on Chessie's face told her otherwise. That had actually been her best effort.

The next girl did cartwheels and handsprings in her bikini—which didn't go so well. She tugged at the bottoms between every move and nearly lost the top during a back handspring. But Elle was impressed that she could do those tricks at all.

"Now we come to number seven," Steve said. Elle walked to the front of the stage. "This is a sweet and sexy suit. What's your name, please?"

"Elle Woods. And I call this the Seal Suit. It clings to your body like a waterproof skin. Like a seal's skin fits a seal."

"Very good. And what is your activity today?"

"Surfing," Elle said.

"All right!" Hunter cheered from the audience. "Rip it up, Elle!"

"Go for it," Steve said.

Elle walked off the stage and grabbed her board. She concentrated on keeping her breathing even, slow, and calm. When she got to the water she ran in, paddled out past the break, and sat on her board to wait for a ride.

A small wave came, but she let it pass, afraid it was too unimpressive. The ocean grew calm. Elle began to panic. She had only a few minutes to demonstrate her activity. What if another wave didn't come? How could she show off her suit?

Nothing came but bump after small bump; they were barely surfable. Steve said through a megaphone, "You have three minutes, Elle Woods! Better take the next wave that comes along."

Elle watched the horizon. Something was coming. It could be good, she thought. She saw it swell and grow as it moved closer. Then she began to panic. Oh, no. It was not just big. It was huge! She'd never surfed anything like it in her short experience on the board. But she had no time left. She had to take it.

The wave loomed up behind her like a monster. Elle took a deep breath, turned around, and paddled.

"Go! Go!" she heard Hunter's and Laurette's

voices among the screams of the crowd. She felt the wave surge under her and popped up to her feet. The wave pushed her forward with terrible force. *Oh, my God*, she thought, looking down at the surf below her as if from the top of a five-story building. *I'm going to be crushed!*

Keep cool, keep your head, and breathe, she told herself. She leaned forward and tried to ride horizontally across the wave. She nearly lost her balance. The crowd gasped. She windmilled her arms and saved herself at the last minute. But the wave was too big for her. She couldn't stay balanced on top of it for long. She bent down and gripped the edges of the surfboard with her hands, holding on for dear life. She kept expecting to tumble into the surf, but somehow it didn't happen. Something kept her on top of that board wobbling and nearly falling and saving herself at the last minute as the crowd screamed in suspense.

At last, the wave crashed onto the shore, and Elle couldn't stay up any longer. She was tossed into the air and splashed into the water as the wave broke just in front of her.

Elle was submerged. The leash of the surfboard tugged at her ankle. She kicked hard and surfaced, gasping for breath.

"She's all right, folks!" she heard Steve shout, to happy cries and cheers from the crowd. She grabbed her board and swam to shore as another, smaller wave broke over her head. She pushed long, wet strings of hair from her eyes. The water had churned and tossed her until her hair was like a tangled clump of seaweed.

Rats, she thought. I guess I lost. Nobody would give a good score to someone who wiped out so spectacularly.

She stumbled sadly out of the water, dragging her board. Hunter would speak out for Sassy, she told herself. And Laurette, if Warp Factor 5 won the Battle of the Bands.

But Elle had really wanted the chance to do it herself. She knew the most about Sassy's situation.

"Here she is, ladies and gentlemen!" Steve said. "Tossed by the waves, taking the worst that the powerful sea has to dish out. Her hair looks like it's been in a blender, but her suit is perfectly in place! She doesn't even have to give one tug on a strap. It hasn't budged a centimeter! Isn't that amazing?"

Elle looked down at her suit. She'd been so busy fighting for balance she'd forgotten about it. But the announcer was right. It hadn't moved a bit. It had stuck to her like her own skin, totally tugless!

The crowd, even the judges, cheered wildly. Hunter offered Elle a towel, and she grinned as she dried herself off, basking in the crowd's attention. Maybe she had a chance, after all.

There were still eight contestants to go. Elle watched them all as they juggled and did karate and played soccer. But by the time the last girl had modeled her suit, the heart of the contest was clear: it was a bikini showdown, and only two contestants had a real chance to win: Nica and Elle.

Chapter 23

"HERE'S OUR final band of the night," Steve said. "Please welcome Warp Factor Five!"

Elle and Hunter clapped and shouted as Laurette, Darren, Mike, Pablo, and Ben, the keyboard player, strode onto the stage. Laurette strapped on her guitar. She looked fantastic in her glittery clothes and makeup. The guys wore ripped jeans and black T-shirts, with plastic leis their only concession to the surf theme. But that was all right; it made Laurette stand out even more.

The Battle of the Bands was wrapping up. Seven other bands had played before the Factor, and they were all great. Some had a reggae sound, others went for a more groovy sixties surfer vibe. Elle knew the Factor would be a little different: surf punk.

Darren took the microphone. "Thanks, surf dudes and dudettes," he said. "We're excited to be here. Here's our first tune. It's not your usual surf song, subject matter–wise. It's not about cars or girls or boards or waves. But it is about the beach, and we think it rocks. It was written by our lead guitarist, Laurette. Hit it, L."

The song began with a speedy, biting guitar riff that reminded Elle of a wasp getting ready to sting. Then Darren half sang, half shouted the words Laurette had written, punk style.

Sneaky secrets
Greedy secrets
Hidden by the sea.
You cheat! You bribe!
You're stealing from us all
Just to build a stupid mall
Or whatever.

Mr. Saunders lies! Yeah!
Mr. Saunders lies! Yeah!
The greed is in his eyes, you can see it.
He says he's helping seals
But he's making shady deals.

Yeah, Mr. Saunders lies.
Believe it.

The beach belongs to nature
And then to you and me
Not only to the rich
With their houses by the sea.
Save Seal Beach for the seals,
Let them come back and live free.
Don't let old Saunders take it
And build illegally!

Mr. Saunders lies! Yeah!
Mr. Saunders lies! Yeah!
The greed is in his eyes, you can see it.
He says he's helping seals
But he's making shady deals
Yeah, Mr. Saunders lies
Believe it!

Elle and Hunter danced the whole way through the song, and so did everybody around them. It was catchy for a political rant. When it was over, the crowd went crazy, cheering, clapping, and yelling for more.

Elle thought of Nica. The way Darren sang,

frankly, it wasn't that easy to make out the song lyrics. But still, it was about Nica's father, and it must have been embarrassing for her.

Elle scanned the crowd for a sign of Nica but didn't see her. She saw Chessie standing off to the side of the stage, arguing with Brett. They'd probably fought through the whole song and not even realized what it was about.

Then Elle spotted Nica up by the road, getting out of her limo. She'd changed into a new outfit and missed the song. Just as well, Elle thought. She agreed with Laurette's lyrics—Mr. Saunders *had* lied—but still, she didn't want to see Nica humiliated.

"You want more?" Darren asked the audience.

"Yeah!" they shouted back.

Warp Factor 5 played the rest of their set. They got the whole beach dancing. When it was over, they took a bow. Laurette's face was shining with happiness, pride, and a little bit of sweat. Elle was proud of her. Darren gave her a kiss onstage. They waved and exited stage right, leaving the crowd shouting for more.

"What did you think?" Hunter asked Elle.

"I think they won!" Elle said. "Not that I'm biased or anything."

Chapter 24

"I'D SAY the first SurfChix contest has been a fantastic success!" Steve Glazer shouted. "What do you say, people?"

The crowd yelped and cheered and surged in front of the stage for the awards ceremony. Elle stood offstage, waiting to hear the final results of the bikini contest. Apparently, the judges were deadlocked and had to go into a special negotiation session to watch a video of the bikini-design competition. All the contestants were jittery, but no one was more nervous than Elle.

"It's so weird that the judges are split," Chessie said. "I thought Nica's suit was a slam dunk. Could they really have liked *my* entry that much?"

"Anything is possible," Elle said.

"While we're waiting for the bikini judges to settle their dispute," Steve said, "let's give out our surfing awards. In third place, with an average score of nine point seven . . . Dave Malkmus of Sydney, Australia!"

Everyone clapped while Dave Malkmus walked on the stage to collect his award. Two TV cameras were focused on the stage; another watched the crowd. Reporters from the local newspapers and TV news clustered near the stage, taking notes as their photographers snapped away. The sun was getting low over the ocean.

"In second place, with an average score of nine point eight, Nica Saunders!"

Elle heard especially loud whistling and cheering from the front of the crowd as Nica, smiling, accepted her prize. Elle scanned the audience, looking for the source of all the noise. *Aha.* There he was, right up in front, clapping his head off and sticking out in this young, hip crowd like an elephant in a tiger cage. Mr. Saunders.

He looked ruddier than ever, as if he'd spent all day in the sun and had forgotten his sunscreen, which he probably had. Beside him, looking unhappy but still clapping proudly for her daughter, was Mrs. Saunders. Interesting, thought Elle.

Nica waved to them and tried to grab the microphone from Steve. "Thank you, Steve. I'd like to thank everyone who helped make this possible: my coach, Kip Carter; my mom; and especially, my dad, Fred Saunders, who paid for my lessons, bought me the best board money could buy, and, most of all, is generously building an animal center right here on—"

"Thank you, Nica." Steve had to yank the mike away from her. "You were great. But I'm afraid only the first-prize winners will become SurfChix spokespeople, and we only have time to hear from them." He looked at Nica as if waiting for her to get off the stage, but she stayed where she was, basking in the glow of the TV lights and smiling at her parents and at the crowd. "So, as I said, thank you, and maybe we'll see you later." He gestured toward a stagehand, who gently pulled Nica off the stage.

"Just when she was going to start promoting her dad's development," Chessie said. "It's too bad. You'd think an environmentally conscious company like SurfChix would *want* to support a man like Mr. Saunders. But I guess it's all about winning."

"I don't think an environmentally conscious company like SurfChix would like what Mr. Saunders is doing to the seal habitat," Elle said.

"I can't believe you're still pushing that line," Chessie said, "after all Mr. Saunders and Nica have told us. I know you're no Einstein, Elle, but I never expected you to be so ignorant."

"No, that's your specialty," Laurette snapped.

"Nica will get another chance to speak when she wins the bikini contest," Chessie said. "I wonder what's taking the judges so long!"

"And now," Steve said, "in first place, with a spectacular average score of nine point nine out of ten, Hunter Perry!"

Elle cheered and clapped wildly as Hunter took the stage. She was proud of him. He looked tall and regal in his board shorts and polo shirt as he graciously accepted the trophy. Elle couldn't help remembering the first time she had noticed him at school. He'd stood on a stage then, too; the handsome star of the basketball team, and just one glance had told her that he was the one for her.

"Wooo! Yay, Hunter!" Chessie shouted so loudly Elle cringed. It was clear whose attention she was trying to get.

"As the winner of the surfing contest, you are now an official SurfChix spokesman," Steve said. "This ceremony is being shown live on national television. Hunter Perry, is there anything you'd like to say to your newfound fans?"

"As a matter of fact, there is," Hunter said. Steve gave him the mike. Nica glared at him, fuming. She must have known what was coming.

"If there's one thing SurfChix has highlighted today, it's the beauty of our beaches and the natural world around them," Hunter began. "It's fine for us to enjoy the coastline by swimming, surfing, or playing on the beach. But we must coexist with the animals around us. This is their home. This place is called Seal Beach for a reason—because it is an important nesting area for the Pacific harbor seal. Please help us fight any development in this area, before we lose the seals altogether! Fight the Saunders Development Company project! Write your representatives and tell them you want no development on Seal Beach! Thank you!"

Hunter had to speak up over the boos and jeers that came from Mr. Saunders alone.

"Don't listen to him!" Mr. Saunders yelled as Hunter left the stage. "He's just a dumb surfer! He doesn't know the facts."

Mrs. Saunders tugged on his arm, trying to quiet him down. Nica just watched the proceedings, simmering. Elle knew she was probably hoping for the chance of a rebuttal. And that appeared to be coming very soon. One of the judges appeared on the stage and whispered into Steve's ear.

"Okay, ladies and gentlemen," Steve said. "The judges have finished their deliberations, and we have the official and final results for the SurfChix bikini design contest." He read from a slip of paper the judge had handed him. "In third place, with an unusual design based on her studies in molecular chemistry . . . guess we'll just have to take her word on that . . . Amanda Abrams!"

Everyone clapped as Amanda accepted her award and walked off the stage. The butterflies in Elle's stomach woke up. This was the moment of truth. If she placed second, that meant that Nica had won.

"In second place, with an original look that cleverly mixes Japanese origami with Lycra spandex . . . Kerry Jackson!"

What? Elle looked at Chessie, who was looking at Nica, who was taking a deep breath and straightening her posture in preparation for accepting her prize. Elle didn't really care that she hadn't come in second—after all, the only way she could get her message across was by winning. Nothing else really mattered. But now Nica had won, and it was *her* message that would spread all over the city, state, and country. And that message had to be stopped.

"I can't believe I didn't get second," Chessie said. "But at least Nica won. There's some justice in the world."

"And the winner of the SurfChix bikini design contest is . . ." Steve paused dramatically, causing Elle's stomach to contract so tightly that none of the butterflies inside were likely to survive.

"—The winner is . . . Elle Woods!"

Elle was stunned. The yelling and screaming of the crowd filled her ears until she couldn't hear anything else. Everything was a blur. She'd won! But how? Why hadn't Nica even placed?

"Go out there!" Amanda Abrams said. "Go get your prize!" She pushed Elle out onto the stage. Elle looked back and saw Nica frozen in place, her jaw hanging open in outrage. Chessie took a step toward her and stopped, afraid to get too close.

"Congratulations, Elle," Steve said. "The judges loved your demonstration. You made a bikini that stays in place no matter what the ocean throws at you. The Seal Suit is the perfect surfer's bikini! The SurfChix company will incorporate your idea into its upcoming line of swimwear. Well done!"

"Thank you, Steve." Elle was still in a daze. She paused to collect her thoughts. She would actually get a chance to make her speech! All the trouble she'd been through was finally paying off.

"Stop the ceremony!" Nica stormed onto the stage in a fury. "Something is not right! I had the best bikini by far. Anybody could see that! I should have won! This isn't fair! Elle must have cheated!" She shook Elle by the shoulders. "Did you bribe the judges? Did you? Is that why they took so long to announce the winner—because you were busy buying them off?"

"No," Elle said, shocked by Nica's outburst. "No, of course not."

"I demand justice!" Nica shrieked. "Unfair! Unfair!"

"Nica, please leave the stage," Steve said.

"No! I won't leave until I get an answer."

"All right," Steve said. "You want an answer? The judges did admire your suit. But one of them thought it looked familiar. The reason the judges took so long to decide on the winners was that one of them suspected you hadn't made your bikini yourself. And when she went online and discovered she was right and showed the other judges how much your bikini looks like the upcoming and yet-to-be released swimwear line of a certain designer named Zola Plunkett, they disqualified you."

"What?" Nica cried. "That's ridiculous! You can't disqualify me! You have no proof."

Mr. Saunders tried to climb up on the stage. "You give my daughter that prize! She won it fair and square!" Mrs. Saunders pulled him back down, but he struggled against her. "Let my daughter speak!" he demanded. "She has something important to say!"

Nica was still going on about what an outrage the decision was and how she'd been cheated out of winning.

"I'm sorry," Steve said. "If you want to lodge a protest, you can do that. But for now, the judges' decision stands. Elle Woods is the winner. She is the official SurfChix spokeswoman. And she has the right to speak." He gave the mike to Elle. Nica lunged for it and tried to grab it away from her. Two stagehands came out and dragged her off screaming.

"Sorry about that interruption, Elle," Steve said. "Take it away, SurfChix spokeschick."

Elle took a deep breath. The TV cameras were pointed at her, their red lights on. She saw Mr.

Saunders at the foot of the stage, red-faced, shaking his fist at her. She saw Mrs. Saunders, nodding encouragingly. And she saw Hunter, giving her a thumbs-up and signing, *I love you.*

That was all she needed. She was ready to pour her heart out.

Chapter 25

"I ENTERED this contest for one reason and one reason only," Elle said. "I have a very important message. It needs to get out. You must listen."

The audience stopped cheering and grew quiet.

"This beach is endangered," she continued. "When I first came here, only a couple of months ago, there was a flourishing seal colony right down there—" Elle pointed down the beach. "Dozens of healthy newborn seal pups and their mothers lived there. The mothers left the pups to find food and came back to feed them. But that was all right, because the pups seemed safe.

"Only a few days later, I walked down the beach and found all the seals gone. All except one pup who'd been left behind." She nodded at Laurette, who had set up a slide projector. Laurette flashed a photo of Sassy along the back wall of the stage. The crowd made a collective sound: "Awwww . . ."

"We call her Sassy," Elle said. "Her mother never came back for her. None of the seals came back, for one reason—because the Saunders Development Company had started building nearby, on protected land. *Illegally*. And that frightened the seals away."

"That's not true!" Mr. Saunders shouted. "She's lying!"

Mrs. Saunders struggled to quiet him down so Elle could finish.

"Mr. Saunders says he wants to build a visitors' center there," Elle said. "That may be true. But that isn't all he wants to build. Show them, Laurette."

Laurette changed the slide, which now showed the plan for a huge development, including luxury houses, a marina, and a yacht club.

"Right now, state zoning makes this development impossible," Elle said, "but that could easily change. If the state senate votes to rezone Seal Beach for residential development, Mr. Saunders will be able to build all of this here, where the seals once nested. Then the seals will never return. And Sassy will never see her mother again."

The crowd gasped. Mr. Saunders wriggled out of his wife's grasp and clambered up onto the stage.

"Sir, you must step down," Steve said, but Mr. Saunders pushed right past him and snatched the microphone away from Elle.

"Are you going to listen to this . . . this *spokeschick's* insane fantasies?" he shouted. "She's just a kid, a little blonde surfer girl in a pink bikini. How can anyone take her seriously?" He tried to laugh, clutching his belly in an attempt to look jolly and nice. The audience didn't buy it. They booed and hissed at him.

Elle leaned in to the mike and said, "I may be a kid, but I know the facts! He's bribing state senators to change the zoning and sell this property cheaply so he can become even richer than he is! It's all totally illegal, and immoral too! And just plain wrong!"

"Doesn't she have an active imagination?" Mr. Saunders said.

Elle tried to grab the mike back. "Reporters: look into the shady deals he's made with Senator Mel Heffernan! Check the records! It's all there."

Even though she hadn't been able to speak

fully into the mike, Elle noticed that several reporters were scribbling furiously in their notebooks. One opened his cell phone and said, "Get me the state senate records right away!"

Mr. Saunders pushed her away. "She's crazy! Go ahead, look into the records. You'll see I'm completely innocent. In fact, my company has a better record on the environment than any other builder in the state. Look it up!"

Elle struggled in vain to get the mike back, but Mr. Saunders wouldn't give it up. Two stagehands tried to help Elle, but Mr. Saunders fought them all off.

Then Mrs. Saunders scrambled up on the stage, with a boost from Hunter.

"Here comes my wife, the lovely Mrs. Saunders," Mr. Saunders said. "She'll back up my whole story. Won't you, sugar pie?"

"Sure, sweet buns," Mrs. Saunders said, a smile plastered on her face. She held out her hand. "Just give me the microphone, and I'll tell everyone the truth."

He handed her the mike and her expression instantly changed from strained obedience to defiance.

"This courageous young woman is absolutely

right," she said. "My husband's company has been lying, cheating, and stealing for years. I've seen for myself what they've done to the wildlife in this state, and I won't stand for it another minute! He'll bulldoze nests of herons, chop down century-old trees, pave over vital marshland . . . anything to make a buck!"

"Mo-o-o-o-m!" Nica screeched from backstage. "No-o-o-o-o!"

Elle was barely able to follow everything as the murmur from the crowd rose to a roar. A reporter barked into his phone: "Scandal! Marla Saunders indicts her own husband! This is a front-page story!"

Mr. Saunders tried to grab the mike from his wife, but she wouldn't give it up. Stagehands and people from the audience flooded the stage. It was chaos. In the melee, someone grabbed Elle and pulled her off to the side. It was Hunter.

"You did it," he said. "The media won't ignore this story anymore. Mr. Saunders will never get away with his plan now."

Nica rushed the stage. "How could you?" she screamed at her mother. "You totally embarrassed me! In front of everyone! On national TV!" She turned to her father and added, "And so did you,

you big, fat liar!" Then she ran off the stage in tears.

"I feel sorry for her," Elle said, "even though she did try to cheat."

"She didn't get away with it," Hunter said. "The best bikini designer won. And now that Sassy's story is national news, I'd bet anything Seal Beach will be saved. Thanks to you."

In the commotion somebody threw a chair, which just missed Hunter's head. He ducked and said, "Let's get out of here."

They slipped away alone for a minute and held hands by the water, watching the sunset. But they couldn't quite escape the lights and noise of the stage. Steve finally got his microphone back. Elle could hear him shouting, "Please, please! Would everybody please calm down and clear the stage? Thank you!"

A few minutes later, peace was restored. "Now that we have *that* under control, it's time for the best part of the day," Steve said. "The beach party! Let's rock out to the surf tunes of the winner of the Battle of the Bands, Warp Factor Five! Playing their new hit, the song that helped them win the battle—'Mr. Saunders Lies'!"

"They won! I knew they would—and with my

new favorite song," Elle said to Hunter. "Let's go back and dance."

Darren sang the newest surf classic while Laurette accompanied him on guitar, Ben played the keyboards, and Mike and Pablo banged away on drums and bass. Elle and Hunter danced the twist and the frug. At the end of the song, Darren said, "I'd like to introduce the newest member of the Five: Laurette. She wrote that great tune you just heard. Also, having her in the band makes five of us instead of four, which is probably a good thing, considering our name. But even more important, she's a great guitarist, and without her we could never have won the Battle of the Bands. Laurette, you rawk!"

Laurette took a shy bow. Elle cheered and whistled along with the rest of the crowd. "Go, Laurette!" Laurette really was a good guitar player; Elle was amazed at how quickly she'd picked it up.

The band ripped into another song. The moon began to rise, and Elle danced in the sand with her handsome, champion-surfer boyfriend. It was the perfect summer night. Best of all, she'd saved Sassy and Seal Beach.

Chapter 26

"LAURETTE, LOOK!" Elle cried. "They're back!"

Every day since the SurfChix contest, Elle had come to the seal cove to look for the seals. A park ranger was posted on the beach twenty-four hours a day to make sure the Saunders Development Company removed all the underwater pilings and anything else they'd begun to build, and that they did not return. For four days, the beach had returned to its quiet, peaceful, natural state.

Elle watched and waited. Would the seals come back? What if they'd already settled somewhere else? What if they'd gone too far from home? What if Sassy's mother had forgotten all about her?

"That's impossible," Bibi said to Elle during her

weekly manicure. Bibi was thrilled that Elle had won the contest. She surprised Elle with balloons, a banner that said ELLE WOODS: BEACH BLONDE, and enough homemade cupcakes for everyone.

"Think about Underdog," Bibi said. "If you were separated, could you ever forget him, even if you never saw him again?"

Elle clutched Underdog protectively to her chest. Tears sprang to her eyes at the very thought of losing him. "No, of course not. I'd never forget Underdog. He's my baby!"

"And I'd never forget Kitty," Bibi said, giving her own Chihuahua a pat. "And Kitty will never forget Underdog, even though they don't live together anymore. So you see, Sassy's mother will come back if she can. It's a mother's way. Just be patient. And please give me your left hand; it's time to trim your cuticles."

As always, Bibi turned out to be right. The seals were back! Elle and Laurette jumped for joy. Elle watched the seals splash playfully in the water and sun themselves on the rocks. Each adult seal had a pup or two with her . . . except for one forlorn-looking seal with white spots and a white face.

"That must be Sassy's mother," Elle said. "Let's go get Sassy!"

They ran to Elle's car and drove to the wildlife refuge. "Paula!" Elle cried. "The seals are back! We can take Sassy back to the beach now."

Paula, the ranger, looked worried. "We can try," she said. "I hope it will work. Sassy has lived here for a couple of months now. I hope her mother will take her back. And I hope she'll be able to readapt to life in the wild."

"She will," Elle said. "I know she will. Please, let's take her back. Hurry!"

Paula put Sassy in her special carrier and drove to Seal Beach in her truck. Elle and Laurette followed. They carried Sassy to the edge of the seal colony. They didn't want to get too close—they were afraid of scaring the seals away again. But very carefully and gently, they let Sassy out of her carrier and into the shallow water.

Elle held Underdog, who watched Sassy sadly. "This isn't good-bye," Elle said. "Sassy will be right here with her mother. We can come by and visit anytime."

Sassy's mother barked from within the herd, and Sassy growled back. For a moment, things between mom and baby seemed tense. Then Sassy flopped into the water and swam toward the colony. Sassy's mother swam out to meet her and led her back into the fold. She nuzzled Sassy, and Sassy nuzzled back.

"Looks like it worked," Paula said, wiping away a tear. "Good job, girls. I've got to tell you, I didn't think this would ever happen. The way things usually go, I thought this beach would be completely paved over by the end of the summer. But you just wouldn't give up. I admire that. And I always like a story with a happy ending."

"So do I," Laurette said.

"So do I," Elle said.

She and Underdog waved to Sassy. Then they left the seals alone to resettle in their home.

Elle and Laurette walked down the beach to rejoin the surfer crowd, all their new friends, and their boyfriends.

"There's still time to enjoy the beach before summer ends," Elle said. "Time to surf and play music and eat Sunrise's veggie burgers."

"What a summer," Laurette said. "So much has happened."

"You became a rock guitarist," Elle said. "And Darren became your biggest fan!"

"I never thought that would happen." Laurette laughed. "And you became an environmental activist. And a gonzo surfer. And a very stylish queen of the bikini babes!"

"That's me," Elle said. "As Bibi said, I am now an official beach blonde."

"And I'm a beach brunette," Laurette said.

"And we're both beach buddies," Elle said. "Wicked."

Here's a sneak peek at

Elle Woods

Vote Blonde

Chapter 1

"It's so good to be back!" Elle Woods said as she stepped through the school doors for the first time that fall. "Ah—Breathe in that delicious school hallway air."

She stopped to take it all in, her first day back at Beverly Hills High: the hustle and bustle, the new faces, the familiar ones, the brand-new clothes . . . And speaking of new clothes, she took pleasure in her new pair of perfectly worn jeans and new lacy blue tank top. It was good to feel dressed exactly right for the occasion.

"Takes you back, doesn't it?" Elle said to her best friend, Laurette Smythe.

"Back to what?" Laurette said. "Tenth grade? That was only three months ago."

"Feels like a lifetime," Elle said. She took another deep breath. "BHH has its own particular perfume."

"Perfume?" Laurette said. "All I smell is sloppy joes and brussels sprouts. I'd rather be at the beach breathing in fresh, salty air."

"Who wouldn't?" Elle said. She loved the beach, and had spent the summer learning to surf, among other things. "But you have to admit there's something exciting about a new school year. We're juniors now. We know what's what. No surprises for us. We're ready to rule the school."

"I guess," Laurette said. She was wearing new clothes too, in a way. Her striped velvet pants and matching jacket had been made in the seventies, but she'd just bought them at a vintage shop the week before. "I miss Darren already. Don't you miss Hunter?"

Darren Kidd was Laurette's boyfriend, and Hunter Perry was Elle's. Both boys had graduated that spring and had just started college. Hunter was at nearby UCLA, and Darren was farther away at University of California, Santa Barbara.

"Of course I miss Hunter," Elle said. "I wish he

could be here—that would make the school year perfect. But since he isn't, I'm going to keep busy. There's so much to look forward to! Cheerleading, and football games, and Homecoming and the homecoming dance . . ."

"So you're going to try out for the squad this year?" Laurette asked.

The year before, Elle had helped transform the cheerleading squad from dishwater dull to bright and shiny, even though she wasn't a cheerleader herself.

"Definitely," Elle said. "Want to come? Tryouts are this afternoon after school."

"No, thanks," Laurette said. "And I think you know why."

Elle nodded. "I understand." Laurette wasn't the cheerleading type. All that pep gave her indigestion. She didn't hold Elle's cheeriness against her, though.

A familiar bologna smell suddenly overpowered the sloppy joes and brussels sprouts. Elle braced herself, because she knew what, or who, couldn't be far behind. Sidney Ugman.

"Elle, you look more stunning than ever," he said. "You're aging so gracefully."

"Aging? She's sixteen, Sidney," Laurette said.

"I didn't mean that you're old," he said to Elle. "I only meant you get cuter every year. Wish I could say the same for every girl at BHH." He looked meaningfully at Laurette.

"I wish I could say it about any of the boys," Laurette said. "Most of them peaked in third grade."

Sidney lived next door to Elle in Brentwood and had had a crush on her since kindergarten. A major crush. Elle tried to be nice to him, but he tested her patience. He was awkward and tubby—and his bologna smell really bothered her. He'd been away at computer camp all summer, which had been like a bologna-free vacation for her nose.

"Who do you have for homeroom this year?" Sidney asked. "Myer?"

Elle checked her schedule. Rats, she thought. She did have Mr. Myer for homeroom. That meant another year of finding creative ways to avoid sitting next to Sidney every morning.

Laurette looked at her own schedule, then Elle's. "We both have Myer. El Comb-over. Room 243." Mr. Myer was known as "El Comb-over" because he was completely bald except for a long lock of hair that he started on one side of his head and wound up plastered over the rest of his skull.

Elle thought it was sad. If only he had cut that thing off and embraced his baldness; he might have been decent-looking.

The bell rang. It was time for the first home-room of the semester.

"Guess we'd better go," Sidney said. "Where will you be sitting, Elle?"

Elle hugged her books to her chest to keep them from getting contaminated by Sidney. New books had such a nice, fresh, papery smell that faded all too quickly. "I'm not sure yet," she said.

"She's sitting with me," Laurette said.

They headed for homeroom to start their new school year. Elle had high hopes for it.

"Ready? Let's go!" Elle chanted a new cheer she'd written for the Beverly Hills Killer Bees cheerleading squad. Last year had been all about basketball, but now Elle was thinking football. New sport, new cheers.

"You don't really have to try out, Elle," Chloe Gaitskill said. "We all know you're good. You totally transformed the squad last year. If you want in, you're in."

The other cheerleaders nodded and murmured in agreement. But Elle said, "No, I want to do things the right way. The official way. So watch me try out, and if you think I'm good enough, take me on."

"Elle is right," Chessie Morton said. "We shouldn't play favorites. We need the best cheerleaders on the squad, not just the girls we like."

This comment was greeted with silence. Chessie was the most enthusiastic yet clumsiest girl on the squad. But no one wanted to hurt her feelings—or get on her bad side—by pointing that out.

Chessie looked up to the top cheerleaders and desperately wanted to be like them. She had followed Savannah Shaw, last year's captain, around like a puppy. This year her idol was Chloe, who seemed to be the obvious choice for captain.

"Thanks for taking my side, Chessie," Elle said. "Wait till you hear this new cheer, though. You're all going to flip!"

She paused, composing herself.

Ready? Let's go! Go, Bees, let's go, Bees, sting those Speedsters in the knees. Flood their engines, pop their tires, cut all their ignition wires. Take the field, run down and score. Touchdown! Touchdown!
Give us more! Go, Bees!

Elle did funky dance moves while she chanted,

ending in a backflip. She'd practiced hard all summer to get it right. Tumbling didn't exactly come naturally to her. She had to work at it. She was better at designing outfits and writing funny cheers.

"Yay!" All the cheerleaders applauded, except for Chessie.

"You've really improved, Elle," Chessie said. "Remember last year, when you couldn't even do a flip? Now you're almost up to our level!"

"I think she's great," Chloe said. "And she's the most motivated girl on the squad. I nominate Elle for captain."

Chessie's jaw dropped. She'd assumed that that honor would go to Chloe. But if it didn't, she wanted a chance at it.

"Chloe, you're so generous," Chessie said. "But you're the best girl for the job, don't you think?"

Chloe shrugged. "It's too much work. I like being a cheerleader, but I don't really feel like making up new cheers or organizing road trips. I say, if Elle wants to do it, let her."

"Maybe we should take other nominations," Chessie said. "Does anyone else have a candidate they want to suggest?"

Chessie stood in the middle of the group,

posing, her hands on her hips. Elle could see that she really wanted to be the captain.

"I do," Elle said. "I nominate you, Chessie."

Chessie seemed a little confused by this. "Don't you want the job?"

"Sure I do," Elle said. "But I want what's best for the team. If the others think you'd be a better captain, then that's what's best."

"I'm sold," P.J. said. "I vote for Elle."

"Me, too," Tori said.

"All in favor of Elle, say aye," Chloe said.

"Aye!" everyone responded, except Chessie.

"What a minute! I didn't get a chance to show what I can do!" Chessie protested.

"We know what you can do, Chessie," Chloe said. "Vote's over. Elle, you're captain."

"Wow!" Elle hadn't expected this. Captain! "I'm honored. Thank you. I promise I'll do my very best."

Chloe picked up the *Cheerleader's Rule Book,* and held it in one hand like a Bible. "Time for your official induction," she said to Elle. "The Cheerleader's Oath. Place your hand on the rule book and repeat after me."

Elle proudly put her hand on the *Cheerleader's Rule Book.* This was a big moment.

"I, Elle Woods—" Chloe prompted.

"I, Elle Woods . . ."

"Do solemnly swear . . ."

"Do solemnly swear . . ."

"To be the best cheerleader I can be."

Elle followed Chloe, repeating everything she said. "To practice faithfully and diligently, to keep my uniform neat and clean, to look my best at all times, to catch the fliers and spot the torches, to give the squad a steady base so we can all fly high. Most of all, I promise to be loyal to my school, my team, and my fellow cheerleaders. A cheerleader is honest and true. Go, Bees!"

"Go, Bees!" the other cheerleaders said in unison, solemnly, with their hands on their hearts.

"Welcome to the squad," Chloe said.

"Thank you," Elle said. "I promise to uphold the principles of the Cheerleader's Oath in everything I do."

"You don't have to go overboard," Chloe said. "Just don't do us wrong."

"I won't," Elle said.

"Sit with us, and watch the rest of the auditions," Chloe said. "There are only two spots open on the squad. You're captain, so you should decide which of the new girls gets them."

Elle sat with the rest of the squad members and watched as girl after girl, mostly freshmen, tried out for those two precious spots. It was hard to decide; several of the girls were very good.

"Thank you, girls," Elle said when the tryouts were over. "We'll post our decision tomorrow morning. You were all great. It's going to be so hard to choose only two!"

She dismissed the girls—taking to the role of captain very quickly—and discussed them with her teammates. Finally, they agreed on two freshmen: Lisi Washburn and Tamila Vines.

"I'll go post the notice in the school building right now," Elle said. "So the girls will see it first thing tomorrow when they come in."

"Elle, have you decided who you want for your cocaptain?" Chessie asked.

"There's a cocaptain?" Elle said. "I didn't know."

"There's no cocaptain," Chloe said.

"But there could be a cocaptain," Chessie said. "Or a vice-captain. Whatever. If Elle wanted one."

"Okay, Chessie," Elle said. "You can be my vice-captain. See you guys tomorrow."

Elle left the gym and went to her locker in the main school building. She wrote out her team announcement in bright blue letters, decorated with gold. (Blue and gold were the school colors.) Then she went to the bulletin board to post the notice.

A boy stood at the bulletin board, stapling a large poster to it. He was pale and doughy-looking, as if he spent a lot of time indoors, which was an anomaly in sunny southern California. He had wire-rimmed glasses and brown hair cut short like a little boy's, even though he was a seventeen-year-old senior. He wore his pants buttoned high on his waist, with his shirt tucked in, but not in an ironic hipster way—just a plain old goofy way.

Elle knew who he was; everyone did. His name was Curt Blaylock. He was the student body president and widely considered the smartest boy in school.

Elle pinned her announcement to the board, then stepped back to read Curt's. It said, REELECT BLAYLOCK FOR PRESIDENT.

"Do I have your vote?" Curt asked Elle.

"Who's running against you?" Elle asked.

"The other candidates haven't been announced yet," Curt said. "But I doubt that anyone else would make a serious bid. Nobody would dare. I'm a shoo-in."

That was typical of Beverly Hills High. In spite

of Elle's best efforts, apathy ran through Beverly Hills High School. Furthermore, the role of student body president wasn't exactly a coveted position. The school president was never cool. And nothing was more important to Beverly kids—most of them, anyway—than being cool.

"Well, if no one runs against you, then I'll vote for you, for sure," Elle said.

"Thanks."

"If you're elected, what will you do?" Elle asked.

"Same as last year," Curt said. "Nothing new. But I do have one big improvement I want to make to the school. I think I'll get a lot of support for it, too."

"What's that?"

"I'm going to abolish all school dances," Curt said. "All of them. And Homecoming will be the first to go."

"What?" Elle thought he must be kidding. How could he abolish school dances? It was crazy. Who would want that?

"What good are they?" Curt said. "Nobody likes them. They're a waste of money—money that could be spent on something way more fun, like a *Star Wars* trivia marathon."

"A *what?*" Elle was stunned. Was he serious?

"I say their time has come and gone. No more dances. And if elected, I'll make sure of it."

Elle was so shocked she hardly knew what to say. No dances? It was barbaric!